LISA THOMPSON

worked as a Radio Broadcast Assistant first at the BBC and then for an independent production company making plays and comedy programmes. She grew up in Essex and now lives in Suffolk with her family.

THE GOLDFISH BOY was one of the bestselling debuts of 2017 and was shortlisted for a number of prizes, including the Waterstones Children's Book Prize. Her stunning second book, THE LIGHT JAR, was chosen as the Children's Book of the Week in the *Times*, the *Guardian* and the *Observer* on publication, and THE DAY I WAS ERASED was Children's Book of the Week in the *Times*.

For Carole

Published in the UK by Scholastic, 2022
Euston House, 24 Eversholt Street, London, NW1 1DB
Scholastic Ireland, 89E Lagan Road, Dublin Industrial Estate, Glasnevin,
Dublin, D11 HP5F

SCHOLASTIC and associated logos are trademarks and/or
registered trademarks of Scholastic Inc.

Text © Lisa Thompson, 2022
Illustrations © Gemma Correll, 2022

The right of Lisa Thompson and Gemma Correll to be identified as
the author and illustrator of this work has been asserted by them
under the Copyright, Designs and Patents Act 1988.

ISBN 978 0702 30159 9

Printed by CPI Group (UK) Ltd, Croydon, CR0 4YY
Paper made from wood grown in sustainable forests and other
controlled sources.

1 3 5 7 9 10 8 6 4 2

www.scholastic.co.uk

THE ROLLERCOASTER BOY

LISA THOMPSON

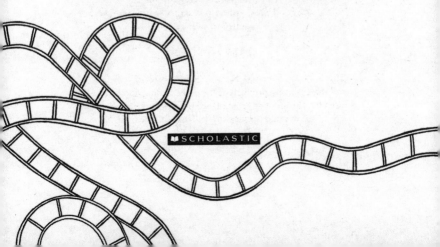

SCHOLASTIC

CHAPTER ONE

"We are not going to the fair."

Aunt Lexie said that life with Dad was like living on a rollercoaster.

"You've had so many twists and turns I bet you don't know which way you're going next," she said as she dished up our dinner.

I knew exactly what she meant, but my little sister, Laurie, didn't understand. She was only six.

"Aunt Lexie? Are we going to the funfair?" she asked. Her eyes were as wide as our plates, which were now filled with sausages, mashed potato and baked beans.

1

"We are not going to the funfair," I said. "You're not supposed to take it *literally*. You are so dumb sometimes, Laurie."

"Todd, don't speak to your sister like that," said Aunt Lexie. She put our dinner on the table and Laurie grabbed the ketchup bottle.

"But I've never been on a rollercoaster before," said Laurie. "*Please!*"

"We're not going to the fair!" I said. "And anyway, you're too small to go on a rollercoaster. They don't let shrimps on scary rides."

"I'm not a shrimp. I'm SIX," said Laurie. She squeezed the ketchup on to her plate and a blob of sauce splattered up and on her school jumper. I'd need to check if she had a clean one in her drawer before Aunt Lexie went home. I didn't know how to use the washing machine so she might need to help me.

I began to cut my sausages up and Laurie got up on to her knees on her seat like she did at every mealtime.

"Laurie, sit on your bottom, please," said Aunt Lexie. "You can't eat your dinner like that."

"But Daddy lets me," said Laurie.

"Well, I'm not Daddy, so you have to go by my rules until he gets better, OK?" said Aunt Lexie. "And let's put these dirty stones away, shall we?"

Laurie liked to collect "stuff". She used to collect feathers, and when she got bored with that, she switched to picking up random pebbles from the garden, claiming that they were valuable fossils. Aunt Lexie brushed the stones into the plastic tub that Laurie used to store them. On the lid in black felt pen she had written:

MY PRESSUSH FOSSILS

I poked at the mashed potato with my fork. There were lumps in it. I opened my mouth to say something but closed it again when I saw how tired Aunt Lexie looked. She had been working since eight a.m. in a care home, gone straight to the supermarket to buy us some food, driven twenty-five minutes to our house, filled the fridge *and* cooked us dinner. Now probably wasn't a good time to complain about lumpy mash.

Aunt Lexie put a plate on a tray along with a glass of water. Apart from using the bathroom, Dad hadn't got out of bed for fifteen days now. I'd been keeping track using the calendar in my school homework planner. He *had* been eating more over the last two days though. When he got his appetite back it usually meant he was starting to feel better.

"I'll just go up and give your dad his dinner and then I'll sort out dessert," said Aunt Lexie. She lifted up the tray and headed to the hallway and the stairs. "It's chocolate cake and ice cream tonight!"

"Chocolate cake!" said Laurie. She waved her fork and a baked bean flew up and landed in her fringe. I picked it off for her and put it on the side of her plate.

"I *love* chocolate cake," said Laurie. "Aunt Lexie always gets us special food when she comes. It's like it's my birthday or something!"

"We only get special food because she feels sorry for us," I said quietly.

She looked up at me.

"Why would she feel sorry for us?" she said.

I rolled my eyes. Sometimes it felt like my sister lived on another planet. She just didn't see what was going on around us like I did.

"It doesn't matter. You wouldn't understand," I told her. She stared at me, her forehead creased.

"Just eat your dinner," I said. "Then you can have some chocolate cake, OK?"

She shovelled a big forkful of food into her mouth, then shuffled up on to her knees again.

"Have *you* been on a rollercoaster before, Todd?"

4

she asked, her cheeks bulging with potato.

"I went on one with Dad once. Mum and Dad took us to the fair but you were really small. You won't remember it," I said.

Her eyes widened. "Did the rollercoaster go really fast?" she asked. "Were you scared? What was it like?"

I remembered the start of the ride. That was almost the worst bit. There was a teasingly slow crawl up a really steep hill and I was so nervous I felt sick. Dad wasn't scared though. He had been grinning and giggling like *he* was the kid, not me.

"Todd?" Laurie said, tugging on my sleeve. "Was the rollercoaster fast?"

"Yes, it was really fast. And there were so many loops that we must have gone upside down at least five times," I said.

Laurie grinned and clapped her hands. "And how high did it go?" she asked. "Did you go as high as the moon?"

"It didn't go quite to the moon but it did go REALLY high," I said. She blinked her blue eyes at me, waiting for more.

"In fact," I said, turning to face her, "it went *so high* that it started snowing! Like it does on the top of a mountain!"

She giggled. "Don't be silly, Todd," she said.

I smiled at her and she turned back to her food, humming to herself as she ate.

Me, Mum, Dad and Laurie had gone to the fairground for my eighth birthday. It was supposed to have been a birthday treat but I remember not really wanting to go. Dad hadn't been well back then, either. He wasn't tired all the time like now. In fact, he was the opposite of tired. It was like he was a human elastic band, pinging around all over the place. Watching him like that made me want to hold my breath in case he suddenly snapped in two.

"Todd?" Laurie said, jolting me out of my memory. I waited for my little sister to swallow some food and carry on. "Do you think Daddy is ever going to get out of bed?"

"Of course he's going to get out of bed," I said, trying to sound cheery. "Now, eat up. Aunt Lexie will be down in a minute to cut you some cake."

She shoved the last piece of sausage into her mouth, then jumped down from the table. I looked at my half-eaten dinner. Thinking about the fair and picturing Mum's worried face that day had put me off my food. Mum was away working in another country right now, that's why we had Aunt Lexie to help us.

But what if Aunt Lexie wasn't around? And what if Dad's other mood came back: the mood he had been in when he made me go on a rollercoaster even after I told him I *really* didn't want to? What if the other dad came back? The one who didn't listen and seemed out of control. That was the one I worried about the most: the elastic-band dad.

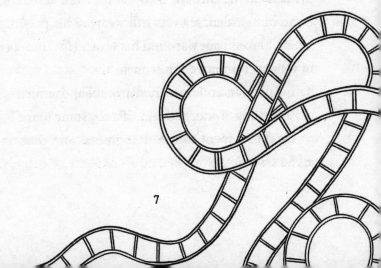

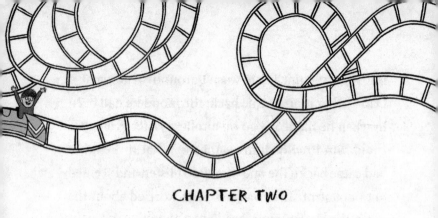

CHAPTER TWO

"Panic Button is here!"

The next morning, I went downstairs to the kitchen and stopped dead in the doorway.

Dad was up. He was standing by the sink with his back to me, stirring a cup of tea as he stared out on to our garden. He was still wearing his pyjamas, which looked baggy around his waist. He'd lost a bit of weight from not eating much.

I walked in and he turned around and smiled.

"Morning, Todd," he said. "Fancy some toast?"

He'd just spent fifteen days in bed and that was all he said?

"Um. I guess so," I said. I put my school bag on the table. "So, you're feeling better then?" I said curtly.

"Much better," said Dad, not looking at me. "I think it must have been some kind of virus or something." He put two slices of bread into the toaster and pressed the lever.

Laurie hurtled into the kitchen and flung her arms around his legs.

"Daddy! You're up!" she said. "Are you taking me to school today?"

Dad picked Laurie up, even though she was getting a bit too big for that kind of thing now.

"You bet I am," he said. I noticed she was wearing her school jumper from yesterday, the one with a tomato ketchup stain on the front. I'd forgotten to check her drawer for a clean one. Dad would just have to sort it out for himself.

I poured myself some orange juice and the toast popped. I went to take it but Dad put Laurie down and came over.

"I can do that for you, Todd," he said. "What do you fancy? Jam? Honey?"

"I'll do it," I said. I put the toast on to a plate. When Dad had been in bed I'd had to drop Laurie off first. Her school was in the other direction to mine so I had to sprint to get to the playground before the bell went for registration. At least I could meet Blake and walk to school with him for a change.

"How about I make you a nice packed lunch?" said Dad. He opened the fridge and stared at all of the food that Aunt Lexie had bought. He probably had no idea what was in there.

"No thanks," I said. "Aunt Lexie gave me some money for school dinners."

Dad got a bowl out of the cupboard and poured some cereal into it.

I watched him cautiously. He certainly looked better, a bit pale perhaps, but not like he did over a week ago. Back then his eyes hadn't looked right. It was as though he couldn't focus on anything properly.

"Your mum is going to call you tonight," said Dad.

"Yay! Mummy!" said Laurie.

Mum and Dad divorced a couple of years ago. They didn't really talk to each other for a while but eventually they seemed to sort stuff out and became friends again. We started staying at Dad's every other weekend and if Mum was away with work. She had a job working for a charity who were building schools in rural parts of Africa. She was home for a lot of the time, but her job meant that if there was a big project, she could be away for weeks. When Mum was away she always tried to video-call us at least once a week if she could get a connection. The last time she'd called, Dad was in bed, even though it was only five o'clock in the afternoon. She hadn't asked where he was so I didn't need to mention it. Aunt Lexie told me that it was probably best not to worry Mum. I think she was probably protecting Dad a bit, as he was her brother. I had wanted to tell Mum, but I was also worried it might make them start arguing again and I really didn't want that.

I finished buttering my toast. Dad was still hovering around, sorting out Laurie's breakfast.

"What happened to your job, Dad?" I asked. Dad frowned.

"What was that?" he said.

I knew he'd heard me. He put a bowl of cereal in front of Laurie. She dived in with her spoon – too interested in her rice pops to be listening to us.

"When you were in bed I heard Aunt Lexie on the phone to Uncle Chris. They were talking about you not going back to work with him. Is that true?" I took a small bite out of the toast and leaned against the kitchen counter.

Dad switched the kettle on and got a mug and the coffee jar out of the cupboard.

11

"Ah, well. It was all getting a bit … complicated, you know? What with Uncle Chris being your mum's brother and that. But you don't need to worry as I've got plenty of other things in the pipeline. OK?" he said.

Dad never seemed to keep a job for long. Uncle Chris, Mum's brother, had his own carpentry company: Sand and Deliver. He'd called Dad about a month ago and offered him a job painting furniture and helping him around the workshop. Dad had enjoyed it when he was there, but two weeks of being in bed had lost him that job, too. It made my stomach feel tight every time I thought about it.

I dropped my half-eaten piece of toast on the plate and picked up my school bag, throwing it over my shoulder.

"I'd better go. I'll see you later," I said. I could tell that Dad was staring at me, waiting for me to look up at him, but I kept my head down.

I walked to the parade of shops not far from home and stood outside the hairdresser's, where Blake and I usually met. I sent him a text.

Walk to school? Todd

I paced around as I waited. Blake and I had been best mates since primary school but we were in different classes in high school so I didn't get to see him as much during the day.

I checked the time on my phone. If he didn't hurry up I'd have to go. I didn't want to be late.

I turned and looked in through the hairdresser's window. They weren't open yet but I could see someone at the back folding piles of black towels by the sinks. I jumped as a squirt of water hit the side of my face and splattered on to the window. The woman looked up from the towels and waggled her fist at me.

"Ah, sorry, mate! I was aiming for the window, not you!" said a familiar voice.

I wiped my cheek with my sleeve and turned around.

It was Blake. He was with Joe Benson, who was in his form and someone who he'd been hanging around with more and more. Blake was holding a sports bottle in one hand and Joe was laughing so hard he looked like he was in pain. I was really hoping to catch up with Blake on my own.

"Seriously! I didn't mean to get you," he said. "I just wanted to make you jump."

Joe was still doubled over. "That was *brilliant*," he

said. "Your face!"

I smiled and brushed the rest of the water off my school jumper.

"No worries!" I said, pretending not to be bothered. "Anyway, come on, we'd better go."

I began to walk in the direction of school and quickly checked the time again on my phone. We'd need to speed up a bit if we wanted to get there before the bell. But Blake and Joe started walking really slowly.

I stopped and turned around. "Are you coming?" I said. "We'd better hurry up or we'll be..." Joe caught up with me and threw his arm around my neck.

"Chill out, P. B., it's all fine!" he said. "We won't be late, and even if we are, so what?"

That was a nickname that Joe had come up with: P.B. It stood for "panic button". He thought I got stressed too easily, and ever since they'd been hanging around together, so did Blake. I hesitated for a moment. I wasn't sure whether to just walk on ahead on my own so I wouldn't get a late mark. But I hadn't talked to Blake for ages so this would be a chance for him, and Joe, to realize I was around again.

"How come you're not babysitting today, Todd?" said Blake. "Was that why you missed my party?"

I briefly squeezed my eyes together. I'd completely

forgotten that Blake had arranged a games night at his house last weekend for his birthday. He looked a bit fed up that I hadn't turned up.

"Ah. Yeah, sorry about that," I began. "I had to—"

"I hope you've been getting paid for looking after a brat. If I had to look after my brother I'd want to be compensated, you know?" Joe said, butting in.

I laughed. "Yeah, I'll get more pocket money next month for sure," I lied. I didn't like him calling Laurie a "brat" but I didn't say anything.

"Hey, Todd. Is it true that your dad is really ill?" said Joe.

"It's not serious or anything, is it?" said Blake.

He was frowning and looked genuinely concerned. I wanted to say something about Dad not being able to get out of bed for two weeks and that I was worried that there was something wrong in his brain that was making him like that, but I wasn't going to risk it with Joe around. He'd only call me P.B. again.

"He's fine," I said. "He's just had a flu thing that wore him out. It was some kind of virus."

"Oh yeah!" said Blake, ignoring me. "Me and Joe are going to the skatepark after school if you fancy it? Meet you at the school gates?" None of us were into skateboarding but we hung around outside on the benches, along with a few other kids in our year. I probably should go as I hadn't seen them in ages, but I wanted to get home as soon as I could to see how Dad was doing. Also, Mum would be calling and I didn't want to miss that. Maybe I could go along for half an hour or so.

"Sure," I said. "But I can't stay long. We've got a video call with Mum later. She's in Africa at the moment. She tries to call us once a week and—"

"Did you see the match last night, Blake?" said Joe. "I can't believe he got sent off! That was *not* a foul."

They began talking about a football match I hadn't seen and I felt myself fading into the background. When we got to school the bell went and they both headed off to their form. I think they'd forgotten I had been walking with them at all. But it didn't matter. Now that Dad was back in action I could start hanging out with them again.

After school I waited by the gates for Blake and Joe, but there was no sign of them. The crowds of kids got smaller and smaller and then I saw my form tutor, Mr Bingham, heading to the staff car park. He spotted me and began to make his way over.

"Everything all right, Todd?" he said. "I understand that your aunt rang the school last week to say your dad wasn't well."

"Yes, sir," I said. I thought he'd go away then, but he just stood there, looking concerned.

"Have you seen Blake and Joe, sir?" I said.

Mr Bingham frowned. "They were just in my maths class and the first out the door as usual. Were they supposed to meet you?" he said

I smiled weakly.

"No, I just wanted to tell them something. That's all." I was about to walk away when Mr Bingham took a step towards me.

"Your dad, Todd. Is he better now?" he asked. I nodded but didn't say anything. Mr Bingham smiled. "That's good. If you ever need help with anything, just ask, won't you?"

"Yes, sir," I said. I turned away and started walking before he had a chance to say anything else. I took my phone out of my pocket and was about to text Dad but I stopped. If it wasn't for him my mates wouldn't have started forgetting about me. He could just worry for a bit and see how he liked it.

Blake and Joe were on the bench in the skatepark with a few other boys from our year. I hurried over but I must have looked stressed as Joe started laughing again.

"Whoa, everybody! Panic Button is here!" he said. "Is there a fire or something? Do we need to call the emergency services?" He was such an idiot sometimes.

"What?" I said. "No, I'm fine. I was just . . . waiting at school. That's all."

They all began to laugh.

"You don't look fine!" said Joe. "You look all stressed out again. Doesn't he, Blake?"

Blake just looked at me. "I didn't think you were coming?" he said. I wasn't sure if I was imagining it, but he looked angry that I was there. He was probably still annoyed about me missing his party.

"I told you I would. Maybe you didn't hear," I said, trying to sound relaxed. I sat on the end of the bench and checked my phone. Dad hadn't noticed I wasn't home yet.

One of Joe's mates who I didn't know started kicking a cola can around. Blake leaped up and joined in and before long I was the only one sitting down. I felt awkward just jumping in so I looked at my phone again.

Dad still hadn't called or texted. What if he was ill again? What if he hadn't managed to pick Laurie up from school? Would he have let Aunt Lexie know?

I jumped up.

"I've got to go now," I said. "Mum's going to call and—"

"Yeah, see ya later," said Blake, not letting me finish.

I turned and rushed off towards home. When I got to my street I spotted Aunt Lexie's car parked outside. My stomach tightened again. Something was wrong. I just knew it.

I fumbled my key into the door. I could hear shouting coming from inside. I burst into the hallway and ran to the kitchen, but it wasn't shouting I'd heard. It was laughter. Dad, Laurie and Aunt Lexie were sitting at the kitchen table, red-faced.

"What's going on?" I asked.

Dad turned and grinned when he saw me.

"Todd! I didn't see you there. Everything OK?" he said. He glanced at the clock. "You're a bit late, aren't you?"

I dumped my bag on the floor.

"Yes I am, actually," I said, not meeting his eyes. "Didn't you wonder why I wasn't home yet?"

"What?" said Dad. "Ah, sorry, Todd. It was just that Laurie said something funny about what happened at school today and I hadn't noticed. Tell him, Laurie!"

Laurie was bright red in the face where she'd been laughing so hard.

"In assembly there was this new teacher," she said, gasping a little. "And his name is. . ." She started to laugh again. "His name is Mr Windrup. But Stanley. . ." Her face creased as she struggled to talk. "Stanley called him . . . Mr Wind-plop!"

Dad fell about laughing all over again.

"Great," I said. It wasn't even funny.

I went to get some juice out of the fridge. Aunt Lexie came over to me.

"You're not that late, Todd. I was keeping an eye on the time and I would have called you if you were any longer," she said. "Is everything all right?"

I nodded. I looked over at Dad, who was now reading Laurie's schoolbook with her. Aunt Lexie saw me watching them and she stepped closer.

"Your dad seems so much better today, Todd. I think we've turned a corner. He's spoken to the doctor and he's back on his medication," said Aunt Lexie. "I have let your mum know what is going on and that he should be fine now, but you know where I am if you need me."

"Sure," I said. I really hoped she was right. I looked at Dad, who was balancing a pen on the top of his lip like a moustache. Laurie was laughing.

Aunt Lexie put my face between her palms and gave me a kiss on the cheek.

"I'm on the end of the phone. Just text or ring me *any* time. OK?" she said.

I looked back at Dad, who now had the end of two pencils tucked under his top lip, pretending to be a walrus.

I agreed with Aunt Lexie. Dad's sadness had definitely passed.

It was what might come next that worried me.

Later that evening, Laurie and I sat together on the sofa when Mum video-called us. She looked happy, tired and tearful all at the same time.

"I miss you both so much!" she said. "How is everything? Are you both OK?"

"Everything is fine, Mum," I said. "Isn't it, Laurie?" My little sister chewed on her thumb as she stared at Mum's face on the screen. She looked like she was going to cry.

"I miss you, Mummy," said Laurie quietly.

"Oh, and I miss you too, sweetheart!" said Mum. "But I'll be back before you know it. It's only a few weeks, really!"

Mum still had another eight weeks in Africa, which didn't feel like soon to me. That was more than the summer holiday.

"Are you all right, Todd? Is your dad OK?" said Mum. "Aunt Lexie texted me and said he's not been—" The screen froze for a moment, then it flickered and started up again. The pause in the call gave me a chance to fix my face with a great big smile.

"He's absolutely fine now, Mum!" I said. "Don't worry." Mum took a deep breath and I saw the huge sense of relief wash over her.

"That's good," said Mum. "Your Aunt Lexie is a godsend. I don't know what we'd do without her! You must tell me if anything is worrying you though, won't you, Todd?"

I nodded and smiled. Then I promised I would.

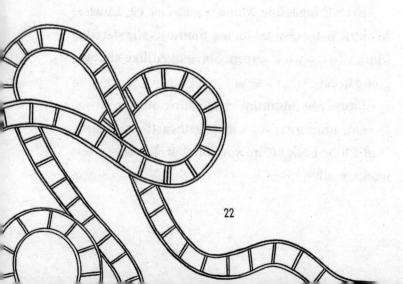

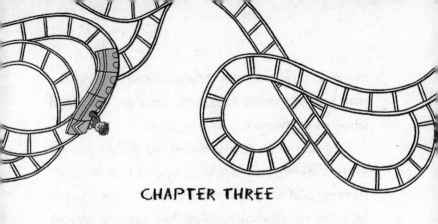

CHAPTER THREE

"Let's put some music on!"

After Dad's fifteen days in bed, a box of white tablets appeared in the bathroom cabinet. His name was on a sticker on the outside, along with instructions saying that he should take one a day. I took a look at the foil packet inside. Each tablet was marked with the day of the week so that he couldn't forget to take one. I decided that I would check them every day, to make sure one disappeared. And they did. Each time I looked another tablet had gone and after ten days I stopped checking. Things slowly got back to normal and it began to feel like the Franklin family were on the straight part of the rollercoaster: the bit at the start before it gets fast and scary, or right at the end when it's all over and you can get off.

Dad dug a new flower bed in the garden and got some work helping a friend who ran a window-cleaning business. He also started running. He began by running every other day, but then he started running every day and even twice a day. Sometimes I wondered if he was doing too much, but his smile was back and he hadn't had to stay in bed so I guessed he was OK.

One Friday night, just before our school half-term holiday, Aunt Lexie turned up at our house with four takeaway pizzas. She was going on a cruise and so we were having a little celebration with her.

"How many countries are you visiting on your holiday, Aunt Lexie?" asked Laurie.

"Ooh, I think four or five?" said Aunt Lexie, grinning. She'd dyed her hair bright red and her nails were painted sky blue. She had been saving up for years to go on a cruise around the Mediterranean with her friend Kim.

"You are going to have such a brilliant time," said Dad. "All that sun, all that lovely food! It's going to be incredible. Incredible!" We were sitting around the table while we ate, but Dad was still walking around with his pizza slice in his hand. I kept one eye on him as he paced backwards and forwards. He seemed jittery to me. I looked at Aunt Lexie but she didn't appear to have noticed.

"When do you leave?" said Dad. I watched his eyes. Were they blinking more than they usually did or was I imagining it? Maybe he was just excited for Aunt Lexie.

"Our flight leaves at five a.m. and then we pick up the cruise ship in Italy. Can you believe it, Dan? I'm going to Italy!" she said. I don't think I'd ever seen her look so happy.

"I know!" said Dad. He finished the pizza and grabbed another slice. He walked back and forth past the sink seven times. I counted.

"Aunt Lexie, can you bring me back an Italian fossil for my collection?" said Laurie. She rattled her tub, which now lived on the kitchen table pretty much permanently. The novelty of picking up random stones hadn't worn off.

"I'll try and remember to find one before I get on the ship," said Aunt Lexie, leaning over and kissing her on the top of the head.

She looked at me and smiled. I smiled back but

looked away quickly. I didn't want her to go and leave us. What if Dad got ill again? Then who could I turn to?

We all helped to clean up after, although there wasn't much to do as we'd eaten the pizza straight out of the boxes.

"Right, I'd better get home and get an early night," said Aunt Lexie. She picked up her bag and we followed her to the doorstep. Dad gave her a big hug.

"Have a lovely time, sis," he said. "You've worked so hard. You deserve this."

When it was my turn for a hug, she put her warm arms around my back and I suddenly felt like I didn't want to let go of her. She pulled away, not noticing my watery eyes.

"I'll see you all in a week!" she said. "Be good and be well! Bye!"

"Bye, Aunt Lexie!" we chorused, and with a flash of red hair, she was gone.

"Let's put some music on!" said Dad. He raced off back to the kitchen. Laurie jumped up and down.

"Yay! Dancing!" she said before rushing off to join him. When I got to the kitchen Dad was connecting his phone to our speaker that sat on the shelf. He flicked his finger across the phone screen and then rock music blasted out. Dad began to pogo around the room and Laurie giggled as she jumped around with him. I felt a heaviness spread across my shoulders.

"Todd! Come on!" called Dad. His eyes were wide as he jumped up and down.

"I need to go and do some homework!" I yelled back. The music was so loud it was hurting my ears.

Dad picked Laurie up and swirled her around as she giggled.

I walked out of the kitchen and headed upstairs, straight to the bathroom. I went in and locked the door behind me. I stood in front of the mirrored wall cabinet and my worried face stared back at me. I opened the cabinet door and took out Dad's white box of tablets. I tipped out the silver foil packets and stared at them, my heart pounding. He hadn't taken a tablet since last Saturday. That meant that Dad hadn't taken any of his tablets for nearly a whole week. I put the packet back in the cabinet and closed the door.

That night I dreamed I was back on the rollercoaster. I was sitting in the front carriage and Dad was beside me. We must have just got on as I could still see a green exit sign. I looked behind us and all the carriages were empty: we were the only passengers. I turned to Dad and was just about to say that I wanted to get off when there was a sound like an alarm and the neck harnesses came down.

"Isn't this fun, Todd?" Dad yelled. His eyes were wide and unblinking and he had a huge grin on his face.

The rollercoaster creaked and groaned as it pulled away and we began to creep really slowly up towards the first peak.

"Woo-hoo!" shouted Dad. "This is going to be great!"

I looked at him. He was laughing to himself.

"Dad? I want to get off!" I shouted above the screeches and strains of the metal wheels against the track.

But Dad just kept looking straight ahead with a vacant, wide smile. It was as if he hadn't heard me at all.

"This is gonna be a big one!" he yelled. "Look how high we're going!"

"Dad? You're not listening to me," I yelled back. My heart was pounding so hard it felt like it was hitting my ribcage. "I want to get off! I want to get off right now!"

But it was as if he couldn't see or hear me. Dad

clapped his hands together in excitement. I looked up ahead. We were nearly at the top now. All I could see beyond was an empty blue sky. This was it. I couldn't get off now. I couldn't turn back.

Dad's hand suddenly reached to hold mine and his wild green eyes met mine.

"Todd," he said, almost calmly. "Brace yourself."

I bit on my bottom lip and squeezed my eyes tightly shut. I felt my stomach lurch as the carriage tipped ever so slowly over the top and—

"Todd! Todd! Wake up!"

I woke up.

Someone was shaking my shoulder.

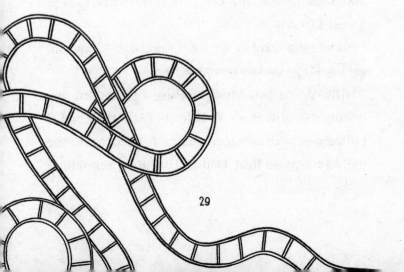

CHAPTER FOUR

"It's not just *any* hotel."

I bolted upright, my heart racing.

"What is it? What's happened?" I said. Dad was
sitting on the edge of my bed. It was still dark outside
and I glanced at my clock. The numbers glowed
green: 4.02 a.m.

"I've got a surprise for you!" said Dad. "Come on,
get up. I'll go and wake your sister."

The stomach-lurching feeling I'd had in my
dream was still there as I slowly got out of bed. I
pulled on my dressing gown and headed out to the
hallway. I could hear Dad in Laurie's room telling

her to come downstairs as well. She was clearly harder to wake up and he came out carrying her over his shoulder.

"What's going on, Dad?" I said, rubbing my face. It had taken me ages to get to sleep last night and then with the nightmare about the rollercoaster it felt like I hadn't actually had any rest at all.

"I'll tell you all about it when we're downstairs," said Dad. He trotted down the stairs carrying Laurie, and I followed. Something was wrong, I was sure of it.

Dad put Laurie on the sofa and she sat there in her unicorn pyjamas with a dazed look on her face. I sat beside her and Dad dived on to his knees in front of us. He was holding our iPad in his hands.

"OK. Right. You know that I've been a bit poorly lately and we've had a bad couple of weeks?" he said. "Well, I had an idea last night after Aunt Lexie left." Laurie gave a really big yawn and her eyes blinked slowly.

Dad carried on. "How about we have a holiday too?"

"A holiday?" said Laurie, waking up a bit more. "To see lots of countries?"

Dad smiled and shook his head.

"No. Not exactly. But how about a trip to …

paradise?" He slowly turned the iPad around. On the screen was a photograph of a grand old building. It had five stories with a turret at each corner of the roof. There were stone steps leading up to two solid-looking pillars and an archway that led to double doors. In the centre of the building was a sign that read in large black letters:

THE PARADISE HOTEL

Beneath the photo of the hotel was a slogan:

Where all your worries disappear.

"We're going to a hotel?" I asked.

Laurie straightened, wide awake now. "A hotel? For real?" she said.

Dad nodded. "Yes! Isn't it brilliant?" he said. "And it's not just *any* hotel. This place is utterly luxurious. I went there with your mum before you two came along and it blew us away."

He swiped through the photos. There was one of a grand reception area with a twinkling chandelier, a bedroom with a bed that must have been five times the size of mine, a ballroom with a shiny black piano and a restaurant with a huge selection of food.

"And it's by the sea!" said Dad. He clicked on some pictures of the hotel at a different angle. There was a wide promenade and then a large sandy beach with sun loungers and umbrellas and a sparkling blue sea. Another photo showed a small funfair by the beach which was packed with rides, including a tall, colourful helter-skelter and a carousel.

I watched as his eyes widened while he swiped faster and faster on the screen. I could feel panic creeping up my chest and making my throat tighten.

"Dad?" I said quietly. He didn't react and just kept staring at the screen.

"Dad!" I said louder. He looked up. "Are you feeling OK?"

He blinked a few times.

"Of course!" He reached over and patted my arm. "Try and relax, Todd. You're such a worrier sometimes."

I frowned at him. Laurie was swinging her legs back and forth and her feet thumped against the sofa.

"Will it be sunny?" she asked. "Is it a long, long, long way away? Do we have to go on a plane?"

Why did she have to be so happy about this?

Dad grinned. "No! That's the best thing of all. It's

not even that far away. I think we could get there in four hours if the traffic is good."

He checked his watch. It was then that I realized that he had the same clothes on that he had been wearing yesterday. He hadn't been to bed. My tight throat was now even tighter.

"When are we going?" I said quietly.

Dad put the iPad down and his eyes widened even more. I swallowed. I had a feeling I already knew what he was going to say but I was hoping I was wrong.

"How about … right now?" he said, grinning. Laurie and I were both silent.

"But we can't go right now," I said. "It's not even morning yet! And … well … we haven't packed."

"You can pack now!" he said, laughing again. "I've got your suitcases. I'll go and put them on your beds."

Dad jumped up and sprinted upstairs. What about his window-cleaning job? Wouldn't the people in charge get angry if he went on holiday without telling them? Also, what about Blake and Joe? I'd arranged to meet them during the half-term holiday. If I wasn't around then they'd never invite me to do anything again.

Laurie looked at me. Even she knew that this was all a bit strange.

"Todd?" she said. Her face looked worried. "Can

you help me pack?"

I chewed on my lip as I listened to the sound of Dad's footsteps upstairs. The floorboards creaked as he moved the suitcases into our rooms.

"Todd?" said Laurie again. She put her hand on my arm and I didn't shrug it off. My head was buzzing. I looked at the clock on the shelf. It was ten past four in the morning. Aunt Lexie would be on her way to the airport now. Was this normal? To get up so early and start packing for a holiday we didn't know we were going on? It didn't feel right.

"Will you help me pack, Todd?" said Laurie.

"All right," I snapped. My head was buzzing with all the worries about how this didn't feel right. But there wasn't anything I could do.

While I was getting ready I checked the bathroom cabinet. The white box of tablets with the sticker was still sitting on the shelf. I looked inside. No more tablets had disappeared. I picked them up and wondered if I should put them in my toiletry bag with my toothbrush and shower gel. But they belonged to Dad. They had his name on them and they had a warning printed on the box which read: "KEEP OUT OF REACH OF CHILDREN". I slotted them back in the gap on the shelf and closed the cabinet door.

It took me an hour to pack, as Mum usually did this kind of thing for us. I filled Laurie's water bottle up at the kitchen sink while Dad put our bags into the car. Laurie was leaning against the fridge, holding on to her tub of "fossils" and twiddling with a strand of her hair. She did that when she was really tired.

"Are you ready?" called Dad, coming down the hallway. He stood at the kitchen door, rubbing his hands together, then came over and scooped Laurie up. She immediately put her head on his shoulder as if it were a pillow.

"Dad?" I asked. "Are you sure about this? I mean, does Mum know?"

"Todd. Enough," said Dad. "You're always looking for something to worry about. You can talk to your mum later this week and tell her all about it. I'm sure she'll be thrilled for you. It's a holiday! How can that be a bad thing? Now just relax, all right?"

I wanted to say that I knew that he hadn't been taking his tablets and if he had, maybe he wouldn't have been up all night, booking a holiday we didn't want to go on. But if I said that then he would know that I'd been snooping on him. And I couldn't deny that he looked happy. *Really* happy.

"Let's get in the car and go, OK?" he said.

He smiled, then headed down the hallway. I took one last look around our kitchen, turned the light off and followed him.

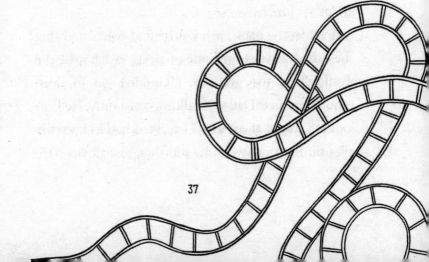

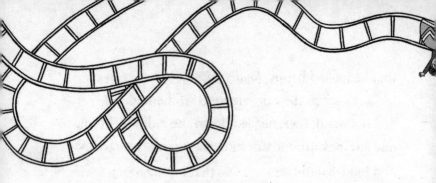

CHAPTER FIVE

"The hotel is broken, too!"

We stopped twice on the way to the Paradise Hotel. Once for Laurie to go to the toilet and once for Dad to buy a large cup of coffee. He also bought three sausage rolls for breakfast and some sandwiches and crisps for lunch.

I sat in the back with Laurie and calculated that she'd had at least an hour of sleep so I hoped she wouldn't be too grouchy. I couldn't get to sleep though because Dad was talking constantly. He kept looking round at me and I felt like I had to keep my eyes on the road when he did that, just in case. He was also very fidgety, adjusting his rear-view mirror, then wiping his finger across the digital screen on the radio, then rubbing his palms against the steering wheel.

"Hey, Todd! Did I tell you that on the beach there is windsurfing and kayaking? How about that then? What do you think?" he said. "Or beach volleyball? That would be good, wouldn't it, Todd?"

I looked outside at the grey clouds and the drizzle. I was about to say that I wasn't too bothered about the beach if the weather was going to be like this, but he started talking over me.

"And the food in the hotel looks incredible! Did I tell you it's an all-you-can-eat restaurant? You can have three desserts if you like. Or five!" he said. He laughed, then carried on talking, barely giving himself time to breathe. I nodded along. Eventually he paused and I quickly jumped in.

"Shall we listen to the radio for a bit?" I said.

Dad slapped his hand on the steering wheel. "Excellent idea!" he said. He put the radio on but he kept changing the station as if he couldn't find one that he wanted to listen to. I sat back and rested my head against the window. The sound of the constant changing channels was annoying, but at least he had stopped talking to me for a while. I got out my phone. I thought about texting Aunt Lexie, but she would be up on the plane now so I'd missed that chance. I could send Mum a message. She was in a rural part of Africa so sometimes it took her a while to receive a text but it would get there eventually. I hovered my finger over her name, but decided against it for now. Instead I sent a quick message to Blake and Joe.

Hi! I won't be able to meet this week after all. Dad is taking us away to some exclusive hotel as a surprise. It looks incredible! I'll send you some pics.

I stared at the text and quickly added a smiley face before hitting send. Hopefully they wouldn't forget me after just one week.

The dim dawn light had now brightened into morning. We drove through a small town and the traffic got heavier so we slowed down. I watched everyone starting their days. I saw three people taking their dogs for a walk, a woman wearing a nursing uniform getting into a car and a teenage boy with a rucksack waiting at a bus stop. I studied him as we got closer. He had his arms folded and he was staring down the road, probably looking for any sign of the bus. I guessed he was a few years older than me, probably around fifteen. I wondered what his life was like. Did he have a dad who took him away on random holidays? Did his mates call him names like mine did? I looked at the message I'd sent to Blake and Joe and wished I hadn't sent it now.

I put my phone away and rested my head on the window. Maybe I should just relax and enjoy the holiday, like Dad said. After all, he was happy and Laurie was excited, so what was the problem?

I must have nodded off because the next thing I knew Dad was talking again.

"Wake up, kids. We're nearly there!"

We were driving through a town which had a handful of shops with their metal shutters pulled down. It was still quite early and the streets were empty.

"Look, there's the sea!" said Dad, pointing ahead. We got to the end of the road and stopped. Ahead of us was an expanse of shingle beach and a churning mass of sea which blended into the steel-coloured sky.

I leaned over and pinched Laurie on the arm. She looked dazed for a moment, then quickly straightened up. Her tub of "fossils" fell off her lap and on to the floor and I reached down and picked them up for her.

"We're nearly there, Laurie," I said.

Dad turned right and drove slowly along the seafront. It was utterly deserted, apart from an old lady in a long raincoat walking a little brown dog. She was clutching a black umbrella and held it tilted against the wind and rain.

I looked out of my window at the waves crashing on to a pebbly beach. I was sure that the photo on the internet had shown a sandy beach with sun loungers and umbrellas. This looked like a different place entirely.

"Look, there's the funfair!" I said. We drove past a tall metal-meshed fence. Through the gaps I spotted some faded signs and something that looked like a carousel horse, but it was propped up against a large green refuse bin. It looked closed but I guessed, like the shops, it was just a bit early.

"Look at all the FOSSILS!" said Laurie, pointing to the shingle beach. Even I didn't want to spoil it by telling her they were just pebbles.

"The hotel is along here somewhere," said Dad. "I remember me and your mum had just the best time here! It was such an incredible hotel. Incredible! I can't wait for you to see it."

I felt a tingle of excitement. If a hotel was named "paradise" then it must be seriously impressive! And I'd never stayed in a hotel before. I shifted to the edge of my seat and peered through the windscreen. Up ahead was a large stone building, staring out to sea. It was the hotel from the website, with the two turrets on each corner. But this version looked very different.

Dad pulled into a space outside and we looked up at the building that would be our home for the next week. Half of the hotel was hidden behind rusty scaffolding that was covered in tattered sheeting. Whoever had been working on the hotel clearly hadn't been around for a very long while.

"Is the hotel broken?" said Laurie.

"Yep," I said. "It's totally wrecked."

Both set of turrets were cracked like eggshells and one of the stone pillars beside the main entrance was split down the middle like a splintered bone.

For the first time that morning Dad was silent. He stared at the hotel, motionless. The car engine was still running.

"Are you sure this is the right place, Dad?" I said, hoping there had been some kind of mistake. "It looks like it's shut."

He remained silent and all we could hear were the crashing waves and a seagull calling mournfully into the sky.

"Daddy? Are we still going on holiday?" said Laurie. There was a wobble in her voice like she was trying not to cry.

I watched Dad's shoulders rise and fall as he took a deep breath. Then he turned around with a big grin on his face.

"Of course it's open! They're just having a bit of building work done, that's all." He turned the engine off and we got out. The rain was coming down heavier now and we didn't have any coats on. Dad went to the boot.

"Here, Todd," he called. "Give me a hand, would you?"

I grabbed Laurie's case and lifted out my own.

"Isn't this exciting?" said Dad. He blinked as rainwater poured down his face. "Let's go and check in, shall we?"

I gave him a feeble smile. Inside I wanted to shout at him that no, I didn't want to check in to this place at all. I wanted us to get back in the car and go home. But Dad headed up the stone steps and pushed his way through the big glass door. Laurie was behind him and I followed with our cases. When I got to the top I put the cases down and looked at a gold-plated sign which had been screwed to the brick wall beside the door. I remembered seeing the quote on the Paradise Hotel website, but this one didn't quite read the same.

WELCOM TO THE PAR DISE HOT L.

here all y ur worries   appear.

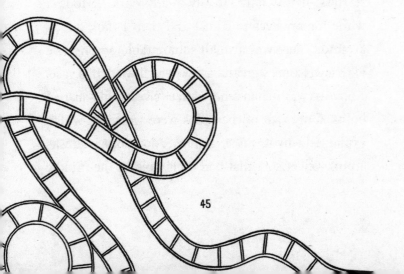

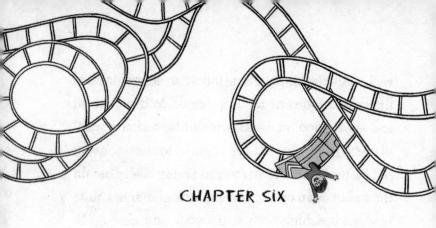

CHAPTER SIX

"Welcome to the Paradise Hotel."

Walking into the Paradise Hotel felt a bit like walking into a haunted house ride at the fairground. For starters, it was dark. Really, really dark. It took a while for my eyes to adjust and then I took a look around. There was a small square table on one side with a welcome sign and a few dead flowers in a vase. Above us was a chandelier with twelve candle-shaped bulbs. Only two of the bulbs were working, which explained why it was so gloomy. Along one wall was a pink velvet sofa that had a big hole in the middle with a silver spring sticking out of it. At any moment I expected someone to jump out dressed as a ghost and shout "boo" at us. There was also a strong smell of burnt toast.

We made our way over to an empty desk. Beyond the desk was an open door that looked into an office. It was piled high with paperwork and clutter. To the right was a staircase and beside that was a lift. Someone had written OUT OF ORDER on a piece of paper and taped it on to the doors. On the desk was a brass bell to get someone's attention. Dad tapped it with his hand and it gave a loud DING.

We waited for five minutes but nobody came. There was a whoosh behind us as the main door opened. A man and a boy walked into the reception, both wearing waterproof jackets and pulling brown-and-gold-checked suitcases behind them. The man completely ignored us, pulled down his hood, walked straight up to the desk and slapped the bell three times.

DING! DING! DING!

"I've just done that, actually," said Dad cheerfully. "I don't think there is anyone here just yet. I guess it's a little early."

The man raised his eyebrows and turned away.

"Patrick. Wait here with the bags," he said. He checked the office and then marched off through a doorway towards where the smell of burnt toast appeared to be coming from.

The boy, Patrick, took hold of his dad's suitcase and wheeled it closer to him as if we were suddenly going to grab it and run off.

"Hello!" said Laurie. "I'm Laurie and I'm six and this is my brother, Todd, and he is twelve." I cringed.

Patrick peered around the edge of his hood at Laurie but didn't say anything. That didn't put her off in the slightest.

"*We're* on holiday," she said. "We're going to go swimming in the sea and to the funfair and eat ice cream and on to the beach to collect fossils. I've brought my collection with me!"

She shook her plastic tub at him.

"Are you on holiday too? Is the angry man your daddy?" she said.

Patrick pulled down his hood and revealed a very smart, shaved haircut and dark eyes. He turned to face her.

"He's not angry, he just gets things done. OK?" said Patrick. I looked at our dad. He was leaning on to the reception desk, his shoulders hunched.

"... and I would advise that you have a team member on your reception desk 24/7. This is no way to run a business." Patrick's dad was marching back through the doorway and he appeared to be giving orders to a small woman with a tea towel tucked into her trouser pocket. She rushed around to the other side of the desk. She had long brown hair which was tied back in a low ponytail. She smiled warmly at us. "I'm so sorry to keep you waiting," she said. "We are having a bit of a ... technical hitch in the kitchen."

Patrick's dad snorted. "A technical hitch? It looked like a complete meltdown to me!" he said. "And from the empty tables in your dining room it doesn't look as though you're exactly rushed off your feet."

Just then an elderly couple appeared from down the stairs. They were each carrying a holdall.

"Oh, Mr and Mrs Johnston!" said the woman behind the reception desk. "We didn't see you at breakfast. Is everything OK?"

The man was staring down at the floor but the woman walked over and placed a key attached to a big wooden fob on to the desk.

"I'm so sorry, Marianne, but we are leaving," she said. The old woman looked quite embarrassed and her eyes kept darting to her husband. "As you know,

Roger and I have been coming to the Paradise Hotel ever since your grandmother was in charge. But it's just not like it used to be."

The woman behind the desk looked like she was about to burst into tears, even though her smile was still there.

"Oh, Mrs Johnston! I'm so sorry to hear that. I can see about refunding you for the nights you haven't stayed," she said, turning to an ancient-looking computer. "Just give me a minute."

"There's no need for that, dear," said Mrs Johnston. "You just . . . you just take care of yourself, won't you?"

The old couple quickly headed to the door and Roger pulled it open with a whoosh. A gust of wind blew in and made some papers on the desk fly up. The woman gathered them together and then quickly composed herself.

"Welcome to the Paradise Hotel!" she said warmly. "I'm Marianne Patterson. Do you have a reservation?" I think she thought we were all together, but Patrick's dad stepped forward and almost pushed Dad out of the way.

"Well, of course we do! We wouldn't be here otherwise, would we?" he said. "Although I must say I am a little concerned. It looks like your guests are leaving pretty sharpish. I do hope it's not a case of rats escaping a sinking ship?" I couldn't believe how rude he was. I looked at Patrick but he was staring at a scuff mark on his trainer.

The woman's smile began to falter and she didn't say anything.

"A reservation for Roland and Patrick Harris," boomed the man. "A deluxe suite with a sea view for a seven-night break, including meals. God help us..." He mumbled that last bit under his breath but we all heard it. Marianne clicked on the keyboard and looked puzzled.

"Hang on ... there must be a suite here that's ... um, up to your high standards, sir." Mr Harris began to tap his fingers on the desk, which made everything feel even more tense. The woman wiped her forehead but then her face relaxed.

"Ah! Here you are, the Lunar Suite." She quickly took a key out of a drawer. "Your suite is on the first floor. I'm afraid the lift is out of order, but the stairs are just to your right. Take a left turn at the top. Have a lovely stay!"

Roland Harris snatched the key and grunted as he walked off. Patrick was still staring at his shoe and hadn't realized he'd gone.

"Come *on*, Patrick," called Roland. "I've got a business call in twenty."

Patrick snapped out of his daze.

"But Dad, it's Saturday! You don't have to work today as well, do you?" he said as he followed him.

The woman behind the desk gave the three of us another big smile.

"Well, hello there!" she said, as if we'd only just appeared in front of her. "I am Marianne Patterson. Welcome to the Paradise Hotel! Do you have a reservation?"

"Yes, we do," said Dad. "Dan Franklin. I booked a family room. For the week."

Marianne Patterson began to scroll through the computer screen again. Suddenly there was a beeping sound, a crackle and then a girl's voice shouted from somewhere.

"SCOUT TO MUM! SCOUT TO MUM! COME IN. OVER."

The voice seemed to be coming from underneath some piles of paperwork on the desk.

"I do apologize," said Marianne. Her face flushed. "Bear with me for just one moment."

She rummaged around, searching underneath cardboard files and pieces of paper, and eventually retrieved a grey walkie-talkie. She took a step back and pressed a button on the side.

"Scout! You are supposed to be in the kitchen. Where are you?" she whispered urgently.

There was a brief crackle and then nothing.

"Scout?" said the woman again. The walkie-talkie crackled then beeped.

"I'm INVESTIGATING!" the voice shouted back. "And you didn't say over. OVER."

Marianne rolled her eyes.

"Just get to the kitchen now, Scout. Please?" she said. Her mouth was all tense and she was clearly trying not to shout. She dropped the walkie-talkie on to the desk.

"I am so sorry about that, Mr Franklin. Let me get you checked in," said Marianne, recomposing herself. She frowned at the computer screen and began to chew on her bottom lip.

"How about room seventeen? Oh no . . . there are no beds in that one. . . Let me have another look." I think she was so absorbed in what she was doing she forgot we were listening to everything she was saying. "Number thirty is nice, but then there's the issue with the toilet. . . Um, I could put you in twenty and twenty-one so you're next door to each other, but then number twenty-eight has that funny smell..."

Dad cleared his throat.

"It was a family room that I booked on your website," he said.

"Ah! Here we go!" said Marianne, beaming at us. "Room number twenty-three! Perfect."

She rummaged around in a drawer and placed the key on the desk.

"Top of the stairs and turn right. Dinner is from five p.m. and breakfast from six a.m. Enjoy your stay!" She quickly turned off the computer screen, then ran in the direction of the smell of burning toast.

I picked up Laurie's bag as we headed to the stairs. Dad was ahead, his tread silent on the thick carpet.

"That girl was called Scout, wasn't she?" said Laurie. "Talking on that thingy. Do you think she's nice?"

"It's a walkie-talkie, and how am I supposed to know if she's nice or not?" I sighed. I had no interest in this Scout, or being here in this hotel for that matter. The tingle of excitement that I'd felt earlier had well and truly disappeared – now I just wanted to go home. We walked up the threadbare carpet. At the top was a long, dark corridor with doors either side. I

looked at the brass numbers on the doors: 8, 9, 10...
We had a way to go yet. The lights along the corridor
flickered as we walked and one went off altogether.

Dad turned around briefly to check we were still
following. He was slowing down before our eyes. I
guessed missing a night of sleep was beginning to
catch up on him.

Laurie stumbled and dropped the handle of her
case. I waited while she picked it up again.

"I wonder what she's investigating," said Laurie.
"What do you think she's investigating, Todd?"

"Who?" I said.

"Scout!" said Laurie.

"How am I supposed to know?" I said.

Laurie was actually quiet for a few seconds, but
I could tell she was thinking about something. I
checked my phone to see if Blake or Joe had replied
to my text about going away. I could see that they'd
both read it but they hadn't answered.

"Maybe she'd like to see my fossils!" said Laurie.

"Who?" I snapped.

Laurie huffed. "Scout!" she said.

"No one is interested in your stones apart from
you, Laurie, OK?" I said.

I kept an eye on Dad up ahead. He had stopped.

"Here we are!" he said. "Room twenty-three."

He put the key in the lock and turned it. The door squeaked as it opened and the three of us stepped inside.

"Oh," said Dad, dropping his bag on the floor with a thump.

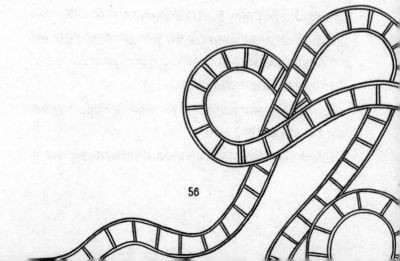

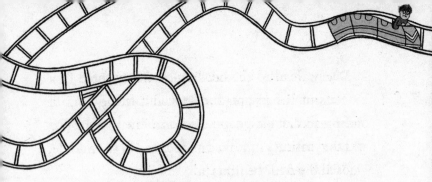

CHAPTER SEVEN

"The carpet hurts my eyes."

Stepping through the hotel door was like stepping through a time machine. Everything was so old-fashioned. The walls were covered in a lumpy patterned wallpaper that had been painted a horrible shade of brown. The carpet was orange with red hexagonal shapes all over it. I couldn't imagine it had ever been fashionable.

"The carpet hurts my eyes," said Laurie, flinching slightly.

I knew exactly what she meant. It made me feel dizzy.

Dad walked to the bed, which was covered in a hideous pink bedspread. It looked like the kind of bedspread that old people died on. He sat on the bed and the mattress squeaked and sagged in the middle. I closed the door behind us.

"What is this?" said Laurie.

On the top of a chest of drawers was a small black box with a bulbous glass front and a loop of wire sticking out of the top. I could see it had a speaker at the back and some knobs on the front.

Laurie went over to it and prodded it with her finger.

"Is it a microwave?" she said.

I went for a closer look. "It's a TV. Like they had in the old days. Isn't that right, Dad?" I said.

But Dad wasn't looking. He stood back up and walked over to the window and looked out at the sea and the rain.

"Dad?" I said, joining him. "Are you OK?"

"This isn't how I remembered it at all," said Dad quietly.

I guessed that he was thinking about when he and Mum were happy together. He looked really sad. In fact, the only person who seemed to be happy was Laurie. She ran around inspecting everything. She opened the bathroom door and when she went in, she gasped.

"Dad! Todd! You'll never guess what?" Her voice echoed. "The bath is PINK and the toilet is GREEN!" She came back out with a big smile on her face and then she opened another door.

"Look, Todd!" she shouted. "This must be our room. There's TWO BEDS!"

I followed her, hoping it might not be as bad as Dad's room, but it was even worse. It smelled old and damp, just like the socks I'd left in the bottom of my PE bag in the last school holiday. We also had a TV that resembled a microwave which was sitting on a dressing table. On the wall was a mirror with a crack down the middle of it. I really, really didn't want to be there.

I went back into Dad's room. He was just standing at the window, silent. It looked like he didn't want to be there either.

"Not exactly paradise, is it, Dad?" I said. He didn't seem to hear me. "How about we head home? I'm sure we could get our money back if we asked on the way out. The woman on the desk offered a refund to that couple, didn't she? If we left now we could probably be home by lunchtime."

I watched as Dad began to rub at the side of his head. At first I thought he had an itch, but he kept doing it. It was like he was trying to erase something from his brain.

"I think..." he said. "I think I need to have a little rest."

He sat on the sagging bed and then lay down on his side. He still had his shoes on but didn't make any attempt to take them off. I stood and watched him for a while, but he just shut his eyes and began to breathe slowly.

Laurie came back in. "Can we go to the beach now, Daddy?" she said. "So I can find more fossils?"

I ushered her back into our room.

"Dad's too tired to go right now," I said. "The early start and long drive have worn him out."

Laurie dived on to one of the beds, which made an awful creaking noise.

"Can *you* take me then?" she said. Her bedsprings squeaked as she moved around.

"No, Laurie. As soon as Dad wakes up we're going home." I checked my phone again for any messages from Blake. Nothing.

Laurie got up on to her knees.

"WHAT?" she shouted. "But we haven't had our holiday yet!"

I looked at her, incredulous.

"Laurie, this hotel is a dump! Can't you see?"

I waved my hand around the room. There was a strip of wallpaper hanging off the wall and one of the curtains was ripped. It looked like a large gaping mouth and the torn material looked like a tongue hanging down.

My little sister's blue eyes flittered around the room and then she blinked at me.

"Well, I like it here," she said. "And I want to stay." She crossed her arms and glared at me. I glanced through the open door into Dad's room. I could see his back rising and falling. It looked like he was asleep. I should probably go in and take his shoes off for him.

"Todd? Did you hear me?" said Laurie. "I'm staying!"

"Whatever, Laurie," I said. "Now be quiet and just read a book or something."

I got up and went back into Dad's room. I heard Laurie huff and then unzip her rucksack. There was the distinctive rattle of her plastic tub full of her stupid stones and then the sound of her little fingers sorting through them.

I slipped Dad's shoes off his feet and put them

down by his bed. Then I pulled the pink bedspread so it was over his shoulders and most of his body. He didn't stir at all.

I stood motionless and watched him sleeping. Dad wasn't himself, I just knew it. And without Aunt Lexie or Mum around *and*, on top of that, being miles away from home, I could feel the panic beginning to rise inside me. It felt like we were creeping up, up, up, to the summit of another rollercoaster track. At any moment we could reach the peak before tipping over the edge and plummeting downwards.

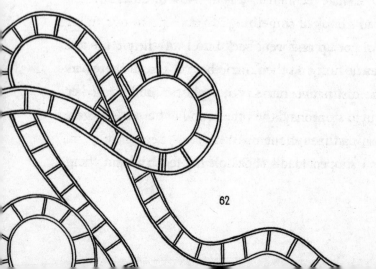

CHAPTER EIGHT

"I think we'll just stay here tonight."

We stayed in our room at the Paradise Hotel for the rest of the day. I hoped a few hours in bed would make Dad feel better and he would drive us home.

I managed to get the TV working in our room, but I could only get one channel and the picture was really fuzzy. We watched three game shows where the contestants had to buy a piece of junk and sell it for more money and then there was a really boring programme about gardening. When dinnertime came, I went to talk to Dad. My stomach was growling.

"Dad? Laurie is really hungry. We both are," I said.

Dad didn't open his eyes. I shook his arm. "Can we just go home? Dad?"

He cleared his throat.

"I'm so sorry, Todd. I think we'll have to stay here tonight," he said. "I'm not up to driving right now. Take Laurie and go and get yourselves some food in the restaurant."

He rolled over without waiting for me to answer.

I stood there and stared at his back. I didn't want to go to the restaurant with Laurie. *He* was the dad – not me! I didn't know how hotel restaurants worked or where we should sit or anything! I found sandwiches that Dad had bought in the petrol station on the way here and went back into our room.

"I'm hungry," said Laurie. "When are we going to the restaurant?"

"We're not," I said. "You can have these." I threw a packet of sandwiches on to her bed. She yawned as she fiddled with the packet. I took it back and opened it for her.

"After you've eaten those, put your pyjamas on, brush your teeth and get ready for bed," I said. She looked at me as she ate, too tired to argue.

After she'd finished eating, Laurie went to the

bathroom to brush her teeth. I began writing a text to Mum. After all, I had promised her I'd tell her if I was worrying about anything.

Hi, Mum. Dad has taken us away for a surprise holiday. It's horrible. I don't want to be here. He went to bed as soon as we got here and I think he's ill again. Can you help?

I stared at the message and my thumb hovered over send. When Mum read this, she would be instantly panicked. She was in a different continent! Plus, she'd be really, really angry with Dad. As much as I was annoyed with him for taking us here, I didn't want to see them fighting again like when they first split up. I deleted the message. It looked like we just had to survive one night here and then tomorrow Dad could drive us home as if nothing had happened. I composed another text.

Hi, Mum. I miss you! Looking forward to talking to you later this week. Hope you're OK. Todd x

The message sent but didn't say that it had been

delivered. Laurie came out of the bathroom, grabbed her small rucksack and climbed on to her bed. From her bag she took out a collection of small, well-worn books. There were four of them and they were in a cardboard sleeve. She tipped them on to the bed and picked one which had a picture on the cover of a boy with his arm around a smiling shark.

"*How to Make Friends with a Shark,*" she read. She opened the first page. "If you see a shark and it looks kind of lonely, why not say hello?"

I lay back on my bed and the springs groaned and pinged. Listening to Laurie put on her reading voice was usually annoying, but for some reason I found it strangely calming. When she got to the end I sat up and told her it was time to go to sleep. I was expecting her to moan, but she was so tired that she just put the books on her bedside table and rolled over.

I got up and pulled a curtain to one side. It had stopped raining but the pavements were shiny-wet. A car drove past slowly, its headlights showing the pools of rain along the road. The sea had calmed down and the waves rolled on to the shingle with a mesmerizing "hush" sound. Our room overlooked the concrete steps that led up to the main door. There was a dim light above the door and I could see that someone was standing there, under the porch. They took a step down and stopped. It was a girl. She was wearing a long dark coat, heavy-looking lace-up boots, and on her face she seemed to be wearing some kind of goggles. They looked like aviator goggles that pilots wore in the old days and they were stretched tightly around her head, making her black hair bunch up at the back. I watched her as she looked left and right. Was she checking if anyone was there? She walked down two more steps and then stopped, staring up and straight ahead. She fiddled in her pocket and took out a notebook, then wrote something down. I followed her gaze to see what she was looking at.

The sea was a swirl of black and navy blue and there were flickers of white light catching the tips of the waves. I looked to where the girl was staring so intently and saw what she was so interested in, high above the horizon in the now clear sky.

She was staring at the moon.

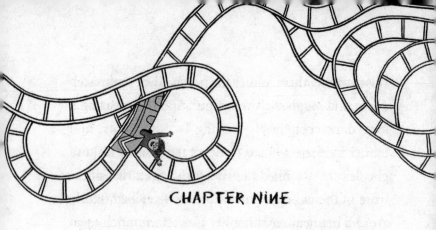

CHAPTER NINE

"When are we leaving?"

It took me ages to get to sleep. The bed was really uncomfortable and every time I moved, the springs made a "twang" like an out-of-tune guitar and a new one would dig into my ribs. The pillow was flat so I tried to make it more comfortable by folding it in two. I must have dropped off in the early hours, which meant when I woke up, it was pretty late.

Laurie was snoring in the bed next to me. My little sister could sleep anywhere. She once fell asleep while queuing for popcorn at the cinema. She just rested her head against Mum's bag and the next minute she was snoring. Mum had to carry her to her seat and she slept through the whole film which was a bit of a waste of a ticket.

As I lay there I looked around the room. The sun was shining through the rip in the curtain, which made the pink edges glow red. It looked even more like a large, gaping mouth. I picked my phone up from my bedside table. The text to Mum still didn't say that it had been delivered, but I had a couple of messages on the group chat with Blake and Joe.

Blake: What hotel are you at? I've prob been there.

Joe: Where are the pics then?

I groaned. Why had I sent that text about coming to a posh hotel? I couldn't tell them where we were staying in case they found out what a dump it was. And there was no way I could send any photos. I couldn't think what to say so I just ignored it. We'd be going home soon and I could make something up about us having to leave. I got out of bed and went to check on Dad.

Half of the pink bedspread was on the floor. He

must have changed out of his clothes in the night as there was a pile on the floor and he was wearing a T-shirt and boxer shorts. His eyes were shut, but something about the way he was breathing told me he wasn't asleep. Not properly, anyway.

"Dad?" I said quietly. "When are we leaving?" His eyes blinked open. He looked at me, then stared ahead at the wall.

"Not right now," he said. He slowly pulled the bedspread over himself so only the top of his head was poking out. "Could you go and find some breakfast with Laurie? Thank you, Todd. I just need a little more sleep."

His voice was muffled. I noticed Laurie was standing in the doorway rubbing her eyes. Her hair was all tangled and sticking up.

"Daddy? Are you OK?" she asked. I ushered her back into our room.

"Of course he's OK. He's just tired, all right?" I said. I didn't want her to start worrying or it would make me feel even worse. Laurie sat on her bed.

"Can we have breakfast now?" she said. My stomach churned with a mix of hunger and worry. I had to go to the hotel restaurant with Laurie on my own. How would I know what to do?

"Get dressed and we'll go and get something," I said. Laurie jumped down off the bed and pulled a long-sleeved striped-blue top and a pair of grey leggings out of her suitcase.

"What about Daddy?" she said. "He needs breakfast too."

She was right. He hadn't eaten anything since we'd stopped at the motorway services yesterday.

"We'll bring something back for him," I said, although I wasn't sure if that would be allowed.

When we were ready we went back into Dad's room.

"We're going to get something to eat now," I told him. His head made the slightest movement, which I took to be a nod. I waited for a bit to see if he was going to talk, but he was silent.

"Come on, Laurie," I said.

I put the door on the latch so that we could get back in without taking the key. As I began to close the door I spotted a sign hanging on a hook on the wall. It read "I'M STILL SLEEPING" in bold red letters. On the back it said, "Hang outside your room and our staff will know not to disturb you". I closed the door behind us and hung it on the handle. If Dad got a few more hours of rest then maybe he'd feel better and

71

then we could drive home. The Paradise Hotel would be like a bad dream.

We walked along the corridor. The lights were still flickering and the weird patterned carpet made it feel like it was moving under our feet. There were no sounds apart from the occasional creak of the floor as we walked. The silence gave me the creeps. Where were all the other guests?

When we got to the end of the corridor we could turn left or right but there weren't any signs to say which way to go. I hadn't really been concentrating when we arrived as I'd just been following Dad. I turned left and was relieved when I spotted the staircase that we'd walked up yesterday. I was guessing that the restaurant was near reception.

"I'm going to have fruit and cereal and juice and sausages and eggs!" chattered Laurie as she trotted down the stairs beside me. "And pastries and bagels and..." She stopped talking. Someone was shouting very loudly in reception.

"This is utterly, UTTERLY ridiculous!" said the voice.

We got to the bottom of the stairs and saw the angry guest from yesterday, Roland Harris, standing by the desk. There was no sign of his son, Patrick, but behind the desk was the woman from yesterday, Marianne. She had a very strained smile on her face.

"You are seriously telling me that you are running a hotel in the twenty-first century and you don't have Wi-Fi?" bellowed Roland Harris.

"I'm so sorry, Mr Harris, but no," said Marianne. "We only have wired internet access in the office, I'm afraid. Maybe this holiday would be a good time to switch off from all of that? A digital detox, maybe?"

She said it kindly but Roland Harris's face turned an even brighter shade of red. It was like his head was being boiled from the inside.

"This is a joke!" he said. "I have stayed in hotels all around the world and this one must rank as the absolute worst. Your pathetic excuse for a breakfast was laughable. The so-called suite we've been given is outdated and embarrassingly inadequate. You are clearly understaffed. This place is the *absolute* pits." He took a breath – his angry ramble seemed to have used up all his puff – then headed towards the stairs. Laurie and I stepped out of the way as he stomped past. He rubbed the top of his balding head as he passed. I could feel the anger radiating off him, like a bad smell. The woman behind the desk sat down in a chair and put her head in her hands. I felt like we had walked in on an awkward situation and I really didn't feel comfortable being there, but Laurie wasn't bothered in the slightest.

"Hello!" she called. She trotted over to Marianne, who looked up.

"Ah, good morning!" Marianne said. Her smile looked more genuine than it had with Roland. "You're the Franklin family, aren't you? We didn't say hello properly yesterday."

Laurie grinned at her. "I'm Laurie and I'm six! And this is Todd and he is twelve," she said.

"It's lovely to meet you, Laurie. I'm Marianne and I am forty-two." Laurie giggled.

"I'm guessing you are both ready for some breakfast, are you?" said Marianne. Her hair was clipped up at the back and a few strands had come loose and hung by her ears.

"I'm starving!" said Laurie.

Marianne smiled at her warmly. "And is your dad coming down too?"

Laurie started to reply, but I quickly interrupted.

"He's not hungry at the moment. But can we, um, take something back for him?"

"Of course," said Marianne. "The restaurant is through those doors and turn right. You can sit wherever you like and then just help yourselves to the buffet."

There was a beep and a crackle and the same girl's voice we'd heard yesterday boomed out of the walkie-talkie which was propped up on the desk beside her.

"SCOUT TO MUM. SCOUT TO MUM. CAN I HAVE THE KEY TO ROOM FORTY-TWO? OVER."

Marianne sighed and pressed a button on the side of the walkie-talkie.

"Scout, we have gone through this. You've been spending far too much time in there and I need you to help me. PLEASE."

"OK. I'll be there in a minute. OVER!" Scout shouted.

Marianne put the walkie-talkie down.

"That was my daughter," she said. "I'm sure you'll meet her before long. It'll be nice for her to see some young people for a change."

Laurie was jiggling around beside me.

"I can be her friend!" she said. "I can show her my fossils. I found every single one and they are really, *really* rare."

Marianne raised her eyebrows and leaned towards Laurie. "Is that so?" she said. "Well, they sound very interesting indeed."

"Come on, Laurie," I said. Marianne gave me a smile.

When we headed off, Laurie reached up and grabbed my hand and began to swing my arm back and forth.

"Get off, Laurie!" I said. I snatched my hand back in case anyone saw.

"But Daddy holds my hand," she said.

"Well, I'm not Daddy, am I?" I said. "Don't do that again, all right?" I put my hands in my pockets. We found the dining room, which looked out on to the road and the sea. There were three other guests. One woman was sitting alone by a tall window and typing on her phone and a young couple were just getting up from their table.

Laurie hurried over to the buffet table that had been set with two large bowls of strawberries and melon, a few apples and bananas, glasses of orange juice, a pile of toast under an orange heat lamp and a jug of coffee.

"Where are the sausages? And the eggs and the bacon?" said Laurie really loudly.

"There isn't any. Just have toast," I said. The sooner we'd all eaten, the sooner we could get out of here.

I put two glasses of juice on a tray, then got some

toast and grabbed a handful of packets of butter and jam. Laurie wanted to sit at a table at the front but I headed to a table in the corner. She followed me and we sat down. The woman on her own got up and nodded to us as she left. I was pleased there was no one else there to stare at us, wondering where our parents might be.

"Can we go to the beach today?" said Laurie.

"No," I said. "What is your obsession with going there?" I didn't understand my sister sometimes. She seemed to live in this weird bubble where she thought everything was all right. Did she think the fact that Dad wasn't able to get out of bed was totally normal?

I looked around the dining room. There was a grand piano in the corner and a huge painting on the wall that was taller than me. It was of a lady sitting at a desk with a pen in her hand. A brass plaque on the frame said it was of "Acclaimed author and owner of the Paradise Hotel, Edwina Patterson". I'd never heard of her. She had pale grey eyes that seemed to be staring right at me. I took a sip of juice and then my phone buzzed. Mum had replied to my text from last night.

Hi, darling. I miss you too! We'll talk in a few
days as usual, yes? See you then. Mum xx

I put the phone in my pocket. I felt bad not telling her
but I was sure that Dad would feel better after he'd
had some rest. And besides, it wasn't like Mum could
just jump on a plane and come back anyway. She was
in a village a two-day journey from an airport.

Laurie was making a mess trying to put jam on her
toast so I took my knife and did it for her. I cut the
toast into four pieces and she smiled at me.

"Thanks, Todd," she said.

Mum hadn't always worked abroad. She'd taken
the job a couple of years ago and this was only her
second trip, but it was the longest one so far. I'd found
out about the job by accident.

It had happened in my last year of primary school.
Mum and Dad had settled into a routine of looking after
us between them and were getting on really well. It was
Dad's turn to have us that weekend and I was allowed
to walk home from school to his. I even had my own
door key on a Luke Skywalker key ring. That Friday I
let myself in and the house was really quiet. Laurie was
sitting on the sofa in the lounge, watching TV. I went
through to the kitchen and saw Mum and Dad standing

in the garden with mugs in their hands. Mum wasn't due to be round until Sunday afternoon to pick us up. They both had their backs to me but the door was wide open so I could hear what Mum was saying.

"... I keep telling myself that it won't be for ever, it's only a three-year contract. And it will be incredible to see the projects first-hand. But I still wonder if I'm doing the right thing."

Dad nodded at her.

"Of course you're doing the right thing," he said. "You've done so well, Kate. I'm so proud of you. The kids will miss you but they'll be proud too." Mum reached over and touched his arm.

I froze. Miss her? Where was she going?

Mum looked all serious for a moment.

"Dan, you've got to promise me something, though," she said. "You've got to promise to keep taking your tablets and checking in regularly with Dr McCartney. You've been doing so well recently. The medication is clearly helping."

Dad nodded but didn't say anything.

"Dan," she said sternly. "Promise me. Things have been so much better, for all of us. Haven't they?"

Dad looked down at the floor and nodded. Then he looked back up at her.

"I promise," he said.

Just then, Mum spotted me.

"Todd! I didn't see you there," she said. Her eyes were wide. "I just popped round because Laurie needed a few more clothes. Are you OK?" She looked at Dad and then back at me. "Is ... is there anything you want to ask me?" I could see in her face that she was trying to work out how much I'd heard. She looked really worried.

"Um, what's for dinner?" I said. Mum looked at Dad and they smiled at each other. They thought their little secret was still safe.

When they eventually told us that Mum would be starting a new job that meant travelling to Africa, I didn't let on that I already knew. I thought if I kept my worries to myself no one could confirm it was true and then maybe it would never happen. But I was wrong. And now I was stuck in a horrible hotel with a dad who didn't seem able to get out of bed while my mum was hundreds of miles away.

After we finished breakfast we went back to the side table to get some food for Dad. Laurie carried an apple and a banana and I quickly buttered some toast and wrapped it up in a napkin. I poured him a mug of coffee and we headed through the dining room, across the reception and upstairs to our room

Dad was still in bed but the light in the bathroom was on so it looked like he'd got up, for a moment at least. Laurie and I stood facing his back.

"We got you some breakfast," I said. I put the toast and coffee on his bedside table.

"I got fruit!" said Laurie. She dropped the apple and banana on to the bed.

"Thanks, Laurie. Thank you, Todd," he said. His face was partly covered by the bedding so his voice was muffled.

He still didn't move.

"I was thinking that once you've eaten we could head home?" I said.

"No!" said Laurie. "Why are we going home? I want to stay!"

I pulled Laurie to one side.

"Stop saying that, Laurie. We can't stay," I said quietly. "Dad isn't feeling well. Can't you see? What is wrong with you?"

She took a deep, shuddering breath.

"But ... but I want to have a holiday and see the hotel," she said. "Can we go and have a look around? Please?"

I looked behind her. Dad hadn't moved. Was he even listening?

"*Please?*" said Laurie. She put her hands together and begged me. It was so annoying, but I knew she would just keep going on and on until I gave in. Sometimes it was just better to say yes and get it over with.

"We'll take a quick look around and then come back here and check on Dad. *Then* we can go home," I said firmly.

Laurie grinned and went to hug me but I stepped out of her way. Undeterred, she threw her arms around my back. "You are the best brother in the world, Todd!" she said.

I shook her off.

"Yeah, yeah," I said. "Whatever."

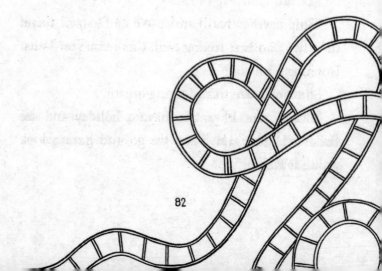

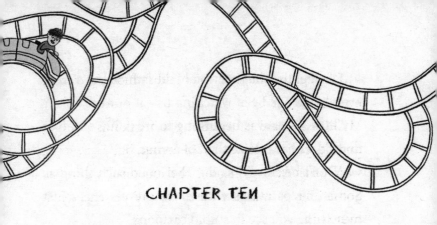

CHAPTER TEN

"I wouldn't go that way if I were you."

I closed the hotel room door and Laurie turned left. We walked along the corridor and she jabbered on and on.

"This hotel is really old, isn't it? Do you think there are ghosts here? I reckon there must be loads. Don't you?"

I didn't say anything.

"*And* pictures of people with eyes that move," she said. "I bet there'll be lots of them, staring at us as we walk around."

I thought of the painting of the lady in the dining room. Had she been watching us eat our breakfast? My little sister was beginning to freak me out. Not that I'd let her realize that, of course.

"Don't be silly," I said. "There's no such thing as ghosts. Or paintings with moving eyes. That's just something you see in stupid cartoons."

We carried on walking past the rows of hotel room doors. I guessed most of them were empty. When we came to the end of the corridor we turned right. I tried to picture the way back in my head but I was already confused. Everything looked the same with the patterned carpet and drab walls. I didn't want to get lost and was just about to tell Laurie that we needed to turn around when I spotted someone up ahead. It was a boy. He was sitting on the floor and leaning up against the wall. As we got closer I recognized him as the boy with the angry dad who had been in reception yesterday. His elbows were on his knees and he was staring at his phone. By the way he was moving the phone around I guessed he was playing a game. Laurie spotted him too and skipped on ahead.

"Hello!" said Laurie. "What are you doing?"

The boy didn't look up.

"Nothing," he said. He stared at the screen, not blinking. The game made loud "CHING, CHING, CHING" noises and he gripped the phone, moving it left and right.

"Come on, Laurie," I said. "Let's go back now."

"Are you lost?" asked Laurie, completely ignoring me.

The phone went CHING, CHING, CHING a few more times and then it made the sound of an explosion and a flushing toilet. He huffed, dropping the phone on to his lap.

He glared up at us.

"What do you want?" he snapped. As usual, Laurie was completely oblivious that he clearly didn't want to talk to us. She had no sense to know when to just back off from people.

"I thought you might be lost," said Laurie. "This hotel is so big it's easy to get lost. Do you not know where your room is?"

"It's here, isn't it?" snarled the boy. He did a backwards nod. On the door was a faded sign that read:

THE LUNAR SUITE

"And it's not a room. It's a suite. There is a difference," he said.

I waited for Laurie to say something stupid about eating sweets and hotel room suites but fortunately she kept her mouth shut. For at least two seconds, anyway.

"Why are you out here then? If your room is right there?" she said. I must admit I was wondering the same. The boy picked up his phone and stared at it again.

"My dad's on a work call," he muttered. "He won't be long, then I can go back in."

We stood there for a while. Even Laurie seemed to be struggling to know what to say. But then she went back to her usual announcement.

"I'm Laurie and I'm six!" she said. I cringed. "And this is Todd and he is twelve."

The boy looked back up. "Yeah, you told me yesterday. So what?" he said.

By this point my sister would have normally got a smile or a kind word from the person she was jabbering on to, but this boy looked like a smaller version of his angry dad. He was wearing a smart checked shirt buttoned up to the neck and dark jeans that had creases down the front like they'd just come out of the packet.

"What's your name?" said Laurie.

"Patrick," he said.

I took a few steps away, hoping Laurie might just give up on her chat and follow, but she just stood there staring at him. My own phone pinged and I took it out of my pocket. It was Blake, and Joe was typing a message.

Blake: Has the hotel collapsed or what? WHERE ARE THE PHOTOS?

Joe: He's hit the panic button! Run!!

Blake: Or maybe it's so exclusive that no photos are allowed?!

I wished I'd thought of that last one. That would have got me out of a hole, for sure. I couldn't ignore them any longer or they'd never give up.

Todd: I'll send photos later. Too busy swimming in the sea!!!!! ☺☺☺

Laurie was leaning over, trying to see what Patrick was playing on his phone, and he was trying to angle it away from her. There was the sudden sound of someone clearing their throat further down the corridor. The three of us turned to see who it was but they quickly ducked away into a recess in the wall.

"Did you see that?" said Laurie. "I think someone is following us! They're hiding!"

Patrick stood up.

"Not exactly doing a good job of it though, are they?" he said. "We can still see your feet, you know!" he yelled. He was right. The toe of a black boot slid slowly backwards out of sight.

"Hello!" called Laurie. "Are you lost?" I gave her a shove.

"Laurie, not everyone is lost, you know."

There was a huff and then a girl's head popped out from the gap. It was the girl I had seen on the hotel steps last night. The one who had been looking up at the moon. And she was still wearing the weird aviator goggles.

"I wouldn't go that way if I were you," she called out. "You'd be much better going back the way you came from. It's far less risky."

"OK," I said. "Thanks for that." I now didn't want to go back as we'd have to go past this strange girl. I put a hand on my sister's shoulder. "Come on, Laurie. Let's keep exploring, shall we?"

We took two steps and the girl called out again.

"Erm, excuse me. Didn't you hear me? I said I *really* wouldn't go that way if I were you."

We turned around. The girl had come out from her hiding place. As well as the aviator goggles she was wearing the same long black coat and laced-up boots that she'd had on last night. Her boots were like the kind that builders wore. I wondered why she was dressed so strangely. Was it some kind of fancy dress?

"Hi, I'm Laurie! I'm six," called my sister. "This is Todd. He is my brother and he is twelve. And this boy on the floor is Patrick. He has been locked out of his room by his daddy."

"I'm not locked out!" said Patrick. "And it's a suite, OK?" He looked the girl up and down. "Why are you dressed like you're in some zombie apocalypse or something? What's with the goggles?"

The girl came closer and began to pace back and forth across the narrow corridor with her hands on her hips. Laurie's head turned left and right as she watched her. I'd never seen anyone like her before. Patrick was right. She was dressed like she had just walked off a film set for a scary movie or something.

Even though she didn't look older than me, she seemed very confident.

"I'm Scout," she said. "I live here."

Laurie let out a squeal. "You're the girl who was shouting on the walking-talking!" she said.

"It's a walkie-talkie, you idiot," I said. Patrick snorted but Scout shot me a look, and it wasn't a friendly one. I felt my cheeks go warm.

"Do you have a sore eye, Scout? Is that why you wear those goggles?" said Laurie. "My eye got stuck together with gunky stuff once and my mummy had to put drops in it to make it better. I had an infection."

I wanted the ground to open up and for me to disappear. My sister was *so* embarrassing. Scout took a long look down the corridor behind us and then back at Laurie.

"These goggles are for protection," she said.

"Protection?" said Patrick. "Protection from what?"

Scout looked directly at him. The goggle lenses had a slight yellow tinge to them.

"Not protection from what," said Scout. "Protection from who."

She began to walk in the direction we were headed. Laurie skipped off beside her.

"Laurie? Where are you going?" I called. I started

to follow them and realized that Patrick was coming too, although he kept a couple of steps behind me.

"We need to go back now, Laurie. Remember we're going home later," I said. "Come on, let's go. We don't have time to mess around."

Scout stopped and put her head on one side.

"Home?" she said. "But you've only just arrived, haven't you? A seven-night booking under the name of Daniel Franklin. That's your dad, isn't it?"

"Yep!" said Laurie. "Daddy is tired now though. He's having a very, very long lie-down." I scowled at Laurie but she just grinned and took a step closer to Scout.

Scout started walking again. I couldn't let my sister just wander off with a stranger so I had no choice but to follow them.

"Your sister is well annoying," said Patrick, catching me up.

I frowned. Even though I thought so too, I didn't like him saying that about her.

"She's only little," I said. "She's just being really friendly."

Patrick laughed. "Friendly *and* annoying," he said.

I was about to suggest that maybe he should stop following us then if he found her so irritating, but

Laurie started asking Scout questions and I wanted to hear what they were talking about. That was the good thing about being little. You can ask any question you like and don't have to worry about looking nosy.

"Is this hotel your home, Scout?" Laurie said. "Do you live here all the time?"

"Yep," said Scout. "My mum owns the hotel now but it was bought by my great-great-grandmother a long time ago. She was a famous author. The Paradise Hotel has been in the Patterson family for over a hundred years."

Laurie was quiet for a moment. None of that seemed to impress her much.

"Do you go to school?" she asked.

"Unfortunately," said Scout. "I keep trying to persuade my mum to let me just work here but she won't let me."

"I love school," said Laurie. "My teacher is *so* pretty. Like an elf."

Scout smirked at my sister and for a tiny millisecond I felt quite proud that Laurie had made her laugh.

"Why are you wearing a coat indoors?" said Laurie. "It's not cold."

"For the same reason as the goggles," said Scout.

"Protection. It's best to keep covered up."

Patrick spluttered and Scout's head whipped round. She gave him a sharp look.

"What *are* you talking about?" said Patrick. "Why do you need protection? It's just a hotel!"

Scout stopped and turned to face him. The three of us watched as she crossed her arms.

"It might be just a hotel through your eyes, but you don't know its deep, dark secrets, do you?" she said. Her dark eyebrows arched as she looked at us.

I felt the hairs on the back of my neck begin to prickle. It had felt like the atmosphere had somehow changed since Scout had turned up.

Patrick laughed and Scout put her head on one side and fixed her eyes on him.

"I'm pretty sure the biggest secret about this place is that it's an actual dump and not as advertised on its website," he said. "It's probably in breach of the Trade Descriptions Act!" I had no idea what he was talking about but Scout just continued to stare at him. He began to look really uncomfortable.

Laurie tugged on Scout's sleeve.

"Who are you protecting yourself from?" she asked. "Can you tell us?"

Scout broke her gaze from Patrick's and stared

down the corridor. She then turned to us, a sly smile on her face.

"Why, from the guest in room thirteen, of course," she said.

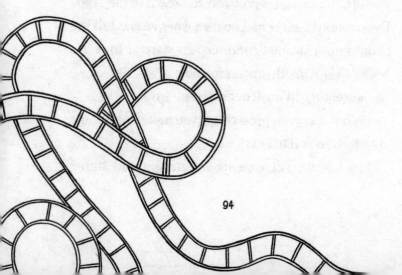

CHAPTER ELEVEN

"A very dark, dangerous secret."

Laurie turned to me. Her eyes were wide open, mirroring her mouth. Her head flicked back to Scout.

"Who's in room thirteen?" she said. "What's their name? Are they dangerous? What have they done?"

Scout's nose screwed up.

"It's not what they've done," she said, a frown on her forehead. "It's what they are capable of doing. That is the concern." She shook her head. "Anyway, I shouldn't have said anything. You are our guests here and ... well, I wouldn't want you to be scared."

Laurie looked like she was about to burst. "But you've *got* to tell us!" she said. "Who is in room thirteen?"

Patrick started laughing. "She's winding you up!" he said to Laurie. "Don't believe a word of it."

This was all getting weirder and weirder. I was definitely *not* going to join in.

"I am not making it up!" said Scout. "If Mum found out that I revealed the secret of the Paradise Hotel to guests she would be really, really mad. We don't want to put anyone off staying here."

"I think you're doing a good enough job of that already," said Patrick. "Just look at the place. It's a dump!"

He elbowed me as if to urge me to join in with him and I frowned at him.

Scout met my gaze through her aviator goggles as if daring me to agree with Patrick. I didn't say anything. I didn't want to get involved.

Laurie tugged on her coat sleeve again.

"Tell me, Scout. Please?" she said. "Who's in room thirteen!"

Scout looked down at my sister's face and seemed to regain her confidence. She lifted her chin and pushed her goggles up on to the top of her head. They left circular indentations around her eyes.

"OK. But you have to promise not to tell anyone what I'm about to tell you," she said. Laurie nodded rapidly. She looked at me and Patrick and we both shrugged. I was intrigued to know what she was going to say, now that she'd made such a big deal of it.

"In room thirteen there is an old man called William Walters," she said. "He's been staying here a very long time but no one knows exactly how old he is."

"Well, that doesn't sound scary," said Patrick. He screwed up his nose and sniffed. "An old man who has been staying here for a while. So what? Apart from him having very poor taste in hotels, that is."

Scout's dark brown eyes narrowed at him.

"When I say that he has been staying here for a while, what I actually mean is, he's been staying here *for ever*." Her voice was hushed and I felt myself shiver.

"What do you mean, for ever?" said Laurie, her voice also hushed.

"What I mean is that he has been a resident of the Paradise Hotel for so long that he now actually lives here," said Scout. "And he has a secret. A very dark, dangerous secret. In fact, it's so dangerous that absolutely no one must know under any circumstances."

Patrick laughed again. "Ah, don't tell me! You're

going to let us in on this so-called secret that no one must know. Am I right? If you are so quick to share a secret with a bunch of strangers then it can't be that serious really, can it? My dad taught me that. It's the secrets that someone *doesn't* want to share that matter."

Scout huffed and straightened up.

"You're absolutely right," she said. "Forget I said anything."

She held her head up and walked off. Laurie glared at Patrick.

"What did you say that for?" she said. "She was about to tell us!"

Scout got to the end of the corridor and Laurie hurried after her.

"Laurie, come back!" I called. I started after them and Patrick began following me. I looked back at him and he raised his eyebrows.

"What's your problem?" he said. "I just want to see how far she's going to take all this rubbish, that's all." I shook my head. He was so rude!

Finally Scout and Laurie came to a halt in front of the room at the end of the corridor.

"So, this guest you have staying in room thirteen," Patrick said, marching up to Scout. "Did you say his name was William Walters?" He folded his arms.

"Yep," said Scout.

"What's his secret then?" he said. "You might as well tell us now."

Scout smiled. She'd played us well and she knew it. The three of us stood around her, waiting. She paced back and forward again, her fingertips pressed together. Then she stopped and turned to face us.

"Many, many years ago William Walters came to stay at the Paradise Hotel. He was an old, old man even back then. But in all the years that he has been staying here, he hasn't aged at all. His hair is long and grey and reaches the collar of his shirt. His eyebrows are thick and white and his skin is so thin it looks like paper. He also has a strange scar on his arm, but he keeps it covered. Just in case anyone sees it."

She stopped.

"Have you seen it?" said Laurie. "Have you seen the scar?"

Scout blinked at her, then nodded slowly.

"Yes. It's on his forearm. It's a semicircular shape and around the edge you can clearly see what made the wounds," she said. "Teeth."

Laurie crept closer to me and her warm fingers clasped on to mine. I didn't let go this time. A guest with a bite mark on his arm? What was she telling us?

"Teeth?" said Patrick, unfolding his arms and leaning forward. "Teeth from . . . what?"

"From an animal," said Scout. "The circumstances around how he got the bite mark are a mystery, but I do know this: many years ago, William Walters made an agreement with a distant grandmother who owned the Paradise Hotel. He offered to pay double the price of his room and she quickly accepted."

This seemed to infuriate Patrick.

"That is utterly ridiculous! Why would he pay too much on purpose? Is he stupid or something?" he said. "You'd never catch my dad paying over the odds for something. He's *really* smart when it comes to money."

I wanted to know more about Scout's story.

"Why did he pay her twice as much?" I asked. Patrick was right. It didn't make sense.

"He paid her more money because he had a condition she had to agree on," Scout said.

She paused and looked up and down the corridor as if to check there was no one listening before turning back to us.

"For one night of the month she had to promise that she would lock William Walters in room thirteen. No matter how much he begged or how much he cried, Edwina was not, under any circumstances, allowed to unlock the door and let him out."

Laurie's fingers tightened around mine and she made a little whimpering sound. Even Patrick was silent.

"On that one night of the month, my ancestor would hear his cries as he begged and begged to be set free. *'I won't hurt you,'* he would say. *'I've changed my mind. Please let me out! I made a mistake!'* Some months she would falter as she heard the desperation in his voice. She would even get so far as to put the key into the lock and almost turn it. But something stopped her from opening the door. The fear of what might happen if she did."

Scout stopped talking and bit on her bottom lip.

"But... but why?" said Laurie. "I don't understand. Why would he want to be locked up? Was he scared?" She was talking so quietly she was almost whispering.

Scout's face looked deadly serious.

"He was scared – in a way," she said. "But it wasn't fear of someone else. It was fear of himself. He was frightened of what he would become." I could see that her eyes kept darting to a door a few metres from where we were standing. On the front of the door was a brass plaque. It said:

ROOM 13

I felt an ice-cold chill at the back of my neck.

"William Walters was locked in his room for one night each month, the night of the full moon, for one reason and one reason only." She pulled her goggles down over her eyes, then stared at us through the yellowing plastic.

"William Walters is a werewolf," she said.

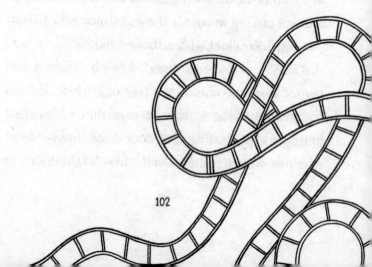

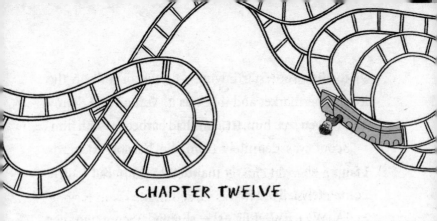

CHAPTER TWELVE

"Don't look directly at him!"

It was quite obvious to me that Scout was one of those people who liked to exaggerate. There was a boy in my form like that: Vernon Richards. He once claimed that he and his cousin, Sonny, had been on holiday to a Spanish island with a famous footballer. He said that they'd played football on the beach with him, had barbecues at his villa and been out on his boat. Vernon had showed off about this for months until Joe bumped into Sonny at the skatepark and asked him all about it. It turned out that Vernon's mum had spotted the footballing superstar buying a carton of milk in the local supermarket and that was it. Vernon and Sonny hadn't even *seen* him, let alone had barbecues with him.

Scout was definitely from the Vernon Richards camp – she was clearly making it all up. But Laurie completely fell for it.

"A WEREWOLF?" she shouted. Scout put her finger to her lips.

"Ssshhh!" she said, looking down the corridor. "He might hear you."

"Oh, don't be ridiculous!" said Patrick. "Are you seriously telling us that you believe a werewolf is living here, in your hotel?"

Scout shrugged. "I'm just telling you how it is. If that worries you, then I'm sorry," she said.

"It doesn't *worry* me," said Patrick. "But you're obviously frightening *her*."

Laurie snatched her hand away from mine and glared up at Patrick.

"I'm not frightened!" she said. She turned to Scout. "Are you wearing those goggles in case the werewolf gauges out your eyeballs?"

Scout smirked. "Kind of," she said.

This was all getting a bit weird and we definitely didn't have time for any werewolf hunts.

"Well, it's been lovely to hear your made-up stories," I said, "but we need to get going. Which way is our room?"

"It's not made up. It's true," said Scout.

"Okaaaaay, if you say so," I said, "but we're going home today so we need to go."

"Yeah, we're leaving too," said Patrick, a snooty look on his face. "My dad is ringing around travel agents right now. I expect we'll end up on the Seychelles again or the Maldives. That's the kind of place we usually go. Not a dump like this."

He sniffed. Scout looked shaken for a moment. But then she focused her attention on to Patrick again.

"If you don't believe me, go and knock on his door," she said.

Patrick looked taken aback. "What? What would I do that for?" he said.

"Knock at room thirteen and prove to me that you don't believe a word I'm saying," said Scout. "We're right here."

Patrick swallowed and his green eyes widened as Scout pointed at the door we were standing in front of.

"I can't just knock on someone's door without a reason," said Patrick. "It's rude!"

Scout folded her arms.

"I'm sure you'll think of something," she said.

Patrick turned to me but I just shrugged. His face flushed pink and he ran a hand through his neat brown hair.

"All right then," he said. "I will. I'll do it right now!"

He walked quickly towards room thirteen and as soon as he got to the door he thumped it with the edge of his fist.

BANG, BANG, BANG!

"I said knock. Not make it sound like there's an emergency!" said Scout. Patrick looked at us, panic on his face. He seemed on the verge of running, but just then the door began to open very, very slowly. Patrick froze with his shoulders hunched up by his ears.

"Keep calm," said Scout in a loud whisper. "Don't look directly at him. If you aren't wearing the right protective equipment he'll be able to see the fear in your eyes. *Then* he might strike."

"So it IS why you're wearing goggles!" said Laurie. Patrick let out a whimper as the door inched open. Scout moved in front of me and Laurie and put her arms out as if she was shielding us. Laurie stepped to one side and I peered over her shoulder so I could see. I felt my heart racing. What if there was some truth in what she was saying? What if this guest really was dangerous? We wouldn't have a chance!

The door finally opened wide enough for someone to step forward on to the threshold. I guess what I was expecting to see was an innocent-looking old man, confirming my view that Scout was talking complete and utter rubbish. But what I saw made me gasp.

William Walters was wearing a dark grey suit and a blue shirt. He was very tall and the suit trousers were far too short for him, revealing a pair of extremely hairy ankles. He had long white hair that reached past the suit collar and rested on his shoulders. His eyebrows were thick and wiry and met in the middle, and the rest of his face was mainly covered with a grey-and-white beard. His skin was thin and beneath his large eyebrows were light brown eyes that were red-rimmed and watery.

"Yes?" grunted William Walters.

Patrick looked up at him and opened and closed his mouth, but nothing came out.

The old man placed a hand up on to the edge of the door frame. Whether that was to steady himself or to restrain himself from lunging towards Patrick, I wasn't sure. His long yellow fingernails slowly tapped along the wood. They reminded me of the claws of a bear that I had once seen in the zoo. As I stared, the sleeve of his shirt edged down, revealing his arm. My stomach did a somersault. I could see part of his scar. It must have been an old scar because it was now just a white line where it had healed, but it was deep and there were some zigzagged shapes on the edge.

"Well?" he boomed at Patrick. "What do you want?"

I held my breath, waiting for him to answer, but Patrick was utterly frozen.

"I ... I ..." said Patrick. He began to shake and then he suddenly burst out, "SORRY! WRONG ROOM!" and turned and ran. He ran past us, along the corridor, and then disappeared around a corner.

The door to room thirteen shut with a loud BANG!

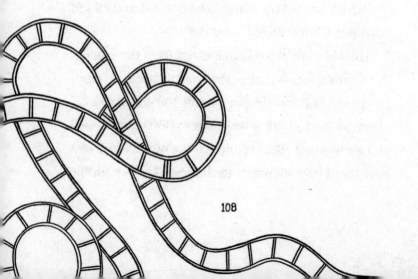

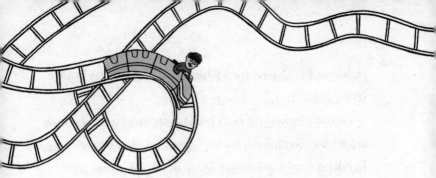

CHAPTER THIRTEEN

"I want to say hello to the werewolf!"

I didn't believe anything that Scout had told us, but the back of my neck was still cold and prickling. William Walters did look very much like a werewolf. And not only that, a werewolf with a bite-shaped scar...

"That was AWESOME!" said Laurie. "Can I knock now? Please!"

"No!" I said. "What is wrong with you?"

"But I want to say hello to the werewolf!" she said.

I turned to Scout, trying not to show how shaken up I felt. "Can you just show us the way back to our hotel room? I've no idea where you've taken us but we have to go back."

Scout chewed on her cheek, watching me for a few seconds. "Sure. Follow me," she said. At last we were heading back. It wasn't long until we came across Patrick cowering in a corner.

"Are you all right, Patrick?" said Laurie, running up to him.

"Of course I'm all right! Why wouldn't I be?" he said. He straightened the collar of his shirt.

"Um, because you ran away?" I said.

Patrick shook his head and gave a false laugh.

"Ah. Yeah. I was just winding you up. I did that for dramatic effect!" He laughed again, but his eyes kept darting back towards the corridor where room thirteen was. We began to walk, Patrick following closely, then Scout turned left and started walking up the carpeted stairs. I didn't think we needed to go up to get back, but I assumed she knew where she was going so didn't say anything.

"What was the werewolf like?" said Laurie. "Did his breath smell of flesh?"

"Laurie!" I said. But even though he was playing down the whole thing, Patrick seemed to take her question seriously.

"I didn't get close enough to notice but he looked incredibly strong. And you saw how tall he was," said Patrick. "And his eyes were amber-coloured! No human has eyes that colour, do they? And … there *was* a scar on his arm."

"You become a werewolf when you get bitten by another werewolf but survive. That's what that scar is," said Scout. "That's his werewolf scar. Did you see it too, Todd?"

I turned my nose up. "Kind of," I said. "But I thought you said it was a bite from an animal? And anyway, just because he had a scar and long fingernails doesn't make him a werewolf!"

Scout laughed to herself. "You noticed his nails then?" she said. "Or claws, should I say. And a werewolf *is* an animal. What else would you call it?"

I wanted to say "made up" but I thought arguing with her was just encouraging all this nonsense so I ignored her. Patrick was chatting with Laurie, replaying everything that had just happened. Surely he didn't believe Scout's story? We were walking along another corridor now but I'd not been paying attention to which floor we were on and it just looked identical to ours.

I walked beside Scout and she nudged me with

her elbow. "It's OK to be scared, you know," she whispered.

"I'm not scared!" I snapped. "I just need to get my sister back to my room so that we can leave, OK?"

Scout flinched.

"Fair enough," she muttered.

I didn't like her calling me scared – it felt similar to how I felt when Blake and Joe called me "Panic Button".

Laurie and Patrick had stopped by a red rope that had been strung across a corridor. Hanging on the rope was a sign that said "STRICTLY NO ENTRY" in bold red writing.

"What's down there?" said Patrick in a hushed voice. The corridor behind the rope was very, very dark. There were no lights or windows.

"That room isn't used any more," said Scout. "It's *strictly* out of bounds to guests."

I took a closer look at the sign.

"And out of bounds to you too, it seems?" I said. Written beneath "STRICTLY NO ENTRY" it read "THAT MEANS YOU TOO, SCOUT" in black pen.

Scout pulled her goggles off the top of her head.

"That's my mum's writing!" she said. "Urgh, she's *so* annoying. She really doesn't like me going down there."

"Why do you go down there if you're not allowed?" said Laurie, leaning against the rope and making the sign swing back and forth.

"I'm investigating something in room forty-two. That's all," said Scout. "Come on. Todd *really* needs to go home."

She said it in a sarcastic tone and we walked the rest of the way in silence. Eventually Scout turned and we headed down a staircase. She stuffed her goggles in her coat pocket. The stairs went on for ever and eventually led to a corner of the reception area. Marianne was behind the desk, talking to a young man in a suit who was holding a large black folder under his arm.

Scout groaned loudly and stomped over to the desk.

"What is *he* doing here?" she said. Laurie, Patrick and I stood awkwardly in the background.

"Ah, hello, Scout!" said the man. "Good to see you again."

Scout folded her arms and scowled at him.

"Back to try and rip off my mum again, are you? Can't you take no for an answer?"

The man threw back his head and let out a ridiculous honking laugh.

"Oh, you youngsters think you are so funny, don't

you?" he said. "No, I'm back for a final look around before we get to the important matter of organizing the paperwork. I'm going to enjoy taking on the Paradise Hotel. It has ... potential." As he spoke he ran a finger along the desk, then inspected it for dust. He brushed his hands on the tops of his trousers and caught my eye for a brief second before looking away. My blood ran colder than it had when Scout had told us about the werewolf.

"Mum won't *ever* sign so you are wasting your time," said Scout.

"That's enough, Scout," said her mum.

"Please don't worry, Ms Patterson. Or can I call you Marianne?" said the businessman.

"Ms Patterson is fine," said Marianne, her voice noticeably colder. I saw Scout's lips twitch into a slight smile.

"But what is he doing here, Mum?" she asked.

Marianne moved from around the desk. "I'm sorry, love, but I've got to do what is best for us. I don't know if you've noticed but I'm not coping so well here," she said. "I know you help during school holidays but the hotel is too much for me on my own. And we don't have the money to employ anyone to help."

"But I don't *have* to go to school, I can just stay

here and work with you," Scout said.

Marianne shook her head.

"You have to go to school, Scout," she said. "We've been through this a thousand times."

The man stepped forward.

"I think you can be proud that you've both tried your very best," he said. His eyes looked downcast, like he was trying to act feeling sad. "Failing is nothing to be ashamed of."

Scout lifted her chin and pinched her mouth together.

"Don't try and act like you care. We're not stupid, you know. You're stealing this hotel from under our feet."

The man shook his head.

"I'm not stealing anything. In fact, I'm doing you a favour," he snarled. "I can't see anyone else lining up to make you an offer. Can you? This hotel is a risky investment. The town isn't exactly a magnet for holidaymakers. And anyway, the business I have is with your mother. Not you." He turned abruptly to face Marianne. "Shall we start our walk-round, Ms Patterson? We've wasted enough time as it is."

Marianne nodded.

"Scout, could you go to the kitchen, please? The

vegetable delivery needs sorting," she said. Scout looked at her mum. You could almost see the anger steaming off her.

"Don't sign *anything*, Mum," she said. "You've got to promise me!"

Marianne gave her daughter a warm smile and put her hand on her cheek. "We'll talk about this later, Scout. You really must stop worrying."

I remembered how Dad had said something similar to me, as if saying it would flip a switch in my head and all my worrying would just vanish. Maybe Scout wasn't as confident as I thought.

"Shall we begin in the dining room?" said Marianne. And they headed off through the double doors.

Scout came over to us. She was visibly shaking.

"Who was that man?" said Laurie. "I didn't like him very much."

"That was Howard Knife," said Scout. She said it like she had a disgusting taste in her mouth. "He's trying to buy the hotel but his offer is so low he's practically stealing it. I just want him to go away and never come back."

Laurie gasped. "But if the hotel is sold then what will happen to the werewolf? Who would lock him up? He would be out there when there is a full moon! He could be really, really dangerous!"

Scout looked at Laurie and gave her a weak smile. Patrick stepped forward and cleared his throat.

"My father is an *extremely* successful businessman," he said seriously. "And I think he would recommend that your mum grab any offer she gets. Howard Knife will probably bulldoze the hotel down and build something else. One thing that Dad says is that you can't be sentimental in business."

Scout bit her bottom lip and tears flooded her eyes. But she didn't cry. Instead she took a deep breath and stood a little taller.

"Right," she said, "I've got work to do. I can't just let my home go to some criminal businessman."

"What are you going to do?" said Laurie. "Are you going to ask the werewolf for help?"

Scout shook her head.

"She's got to check the vegetable delivery, hasn't she? Her mum just said so," said Patrick.

"I'm not checking any vegetables. I've got more important tasks than that. Like a mystery to solve," she said. She straightened up and brushed her fringe out of her eyes.

"A mystery?" said Laurie. "What mystery?"

Scout frowned as if she was unsure of herself for a moment.

"Oh, it's just something I've been working on. To do with room forty-two," she said. "It's probably nothing, but I've got to try. For the sake of the hotel."

My little sister's eyebrows were so high they were nearly off her forehead.

"Is room forty-two in the forbidden corridor?" she said. "Where the red rope is?"

"Yes," said Scout. "But it's out of bounds for guests. And, well, me, I guess."

"Can *we* help Scout with the mystery in room forty-two, Todd? Please?" she said.

"No, Laurie. We can't," I said.

"It's fine, Laurie," said Scout kindly. For a moment she really looked and sounded like her mum.

"I'm sorry we can't help, Scout," I said. "We'll be leaving soon but, you know, good luck with whatever it is."

"No problem," said Scout. "You probably wouldn't be able to help anyway."

I nodded, wondering for a split second what the mystery actually was.

"Yeah, I'm sorry I can't help either," said Patrick, suddenly stepping forward even though he wasn't included in the conversation. "I'd better go back to our suite and see where we are jetting off to next."

Scout held her head up high, although I thought she looked a bit hurt that we were so keen to leave. Laurie was glaring at me.

"Todd, PLEASE!" she begged.

"No, Laurie!" I shouted. She folded her arms in protest, then reluctantly followed me to the stairs.

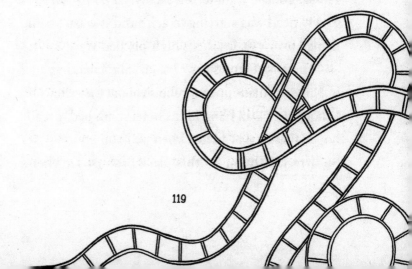

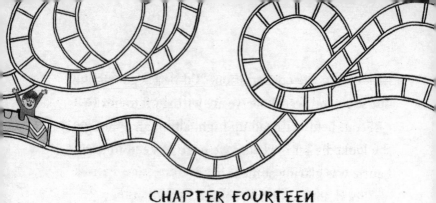

CHAPTER FOURTEEN

"I'll see you later, losers!"

Laurie began whingeing as soon as we headed off.

"But *why* can't we help Scout?" she said. "It would be a real-life adventure! We never go on adventures. Please, Todd. I want to solve a mystery. *PLEASE!*"

My head was starting to ache and it wasn't being helped by my little sister's high-pitched voice.

"There isn't a mystery," I said. "She's making it all up! Like she made up that rubbish about the werewolf." I thought of Dad lying in his hotel room bed. I really hoped that he'd be better when we got there.

"I reckon living in this place has just sent her a

bit ... you know," said Patrick, circling his finger by his forehead. "I mean, who actually believes in that stuff?" He seemed to have forgotten how terrified he was when he knocked on the door of room thirteen.

We reached the top of the stairs where Patrick needed to turn off to get to his room, or suite.

"I'll see you later, losers!" he said. "I'll think of you when I'm lying on an exotic beach somewhere!" He did a weird wave at us, then trotted off down the hallway.

Laurie stood in my way, her face scrunched up. I knew she was not going to give up whingeing yet.

"*Why* can't we go and help Scout!" she said. "What is *wrong* with you?"

I turned and grabbed hold of her arm.

"What is wrong with me is that I have to be responsible for you and I don't want to be!" I snapped.

She pulled her arm away and I could tell that she was trying not to cry.

"You're just too little to understand what is going on, OK?" I said, feeling a bit bad. "Just leave it and do what I tell you."

My sister scowled at me.

"I might be little but I'm not stupid," she said. "I found all of those fossils, didn't I? That's not something anyone can do! They're rare!"

I could feel myself begin to erupt.

"Don't be stupid, Laurie. They're just stones from the garden! They are not fossils! We just agree with you because ... because you're a little kid!"

Laurie's face flinched as if I'd slapped her. And then she turned and ran off. I stormed off towards our room. I'd had enough. Laurie was not my responsibility.

When I got back to the room Dad would be waiting with the bags all packed and I would tell him how selfish she was being. We'd find Laurie and he would tell her off for giving me a hard time, then we'd go home and this whole nightmare would be over.

I got to our room. The "I'm still sleeping" sign was still on the door. I opened it, expecting to see Dad sitting with our bags, ready to jump up with a smile. But he wasn't. The room was still gloomy, the curtains still drawn, and under the covers was a Dad-shaped lump.

"Dad?" I said, standing by the bed. "I'm back. Are you OK?"

I looked at the breakfast we'd left for him. It looked like a quarter of the coffee had been drunk, but nothing else had been touched. Dad's eyes blinked open and he very slowly turned his head.

"Todd?" he said. "Are you both OK?"

"Yes, but can we just go home?" I said. "We could call for a taxi if you can't drive. Please?" My voice wobbled and I disguised it as a cough.

"We ... we can't right now," said Dad. "Please don't worry. I'm just really, really tired." He closed his eyes again.

I bit down on my lip so I wouldn't cry. Then I went into our room and got my phone out.

I wasn't sure what to do but I knew that we needed help. Maybe Aunt Lexie would have an idea. I began to type a text message. I knew she couldn't come and get us but she might have an idea of what to do. Or maybe she'd know someone who could come and pick us up. I stared at the screen. I didn't want to ruin her special holiday so I'd have to write in a way that wouldn't worry her.

Hi, Aunt Lexie! I hope you're having a nice time? I'm sorry to bother you but Dad took us to a hotel and now he's not feeling very well. It's nothing serious! But I don't know what

I reread what I'd written. I wasn't sure if she'd be able

to tell that I was trying to make things sounds less serious. Maybe I should just be honest with her and tell her I was scared?

I deleted what I'd written and decided to start again.

Hi, Aunt Lexie. I need your help.

I stopped again. Something caught my eye. There was something hidden under Laurie's pillow, making a big bulge. I got up to take a look. I pulled the pillow out of the way to reveal her plastic tub with the label on the lid:

MY PRESSUSH FOSSILS

I stared at the tub. She must have put them under her pillow this morning to keep them safe. Now that my anger had faded it was quickly replaced with a sense of panic. Laurie was wandering around the hotel with its dark, twisting corridors and resident werewolf on her own and *I* was supposed to be looking after her.

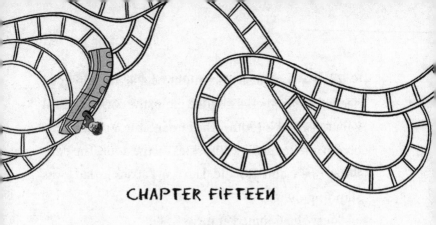

CHAPTER FiFTEEN

"I'm a human satnav."

I put my phone into my pocket and headed back out into the corridor, closing the door behind me. Dad didn't even look up. My text message to Aunt Lexie would just have to wait. I looked around. There was no sign of Laurie but I knew exactly where she was heading: room forty-two. Or at least, she would be trying to head there. There was no way she'd know which way to go and neither did I. I wasn't sure whether to turn right and towards the stairs and down to reception – or would Laurie have chosen the other way, towards where the "werewolf" lived?

I knew someone who might be able to help but I needed to be quick. I hurried along the corridor until I got to Patrick's room – the Lunar Suite. I took a deep breath and tapped my knuckles on the door. The door flung open and Roland Harris, Patrick's dad, was standing there.

"Yes?" he boomed at me.

"Um. Is Patrick there, please?" I asked. Patrick's head peeked around the corner from inside the room. He looked very surprised to see me standing at his door.

"Hi, Patrick," I said. "I know you're leaving soon but—"

"What?" shouted Roland. "Leaving? But I have this suite booked for a week! What are you talking about? Do you work here?"

"No. I ... just, I didn't think you liked it here," I said. My eyes darted back to Patrick, who was staring at the floor. "I thought you were heading abroad. To the Seychelles or something. I must have ... misunderstood."

Patrick looked up and I gave him a weak smile.

"Chance would be a fine thing!" said Roland. "I have business dealings in the area and it's my turn to have him. Little did I know it was a school holiday. His mum failed to tell me about that, didn't she?"

He stared at me as if he actually wanted me to say something. I stayed silent.

"Apparently it's all right for her to go swanning off to the south of France with her best friend, but if I need to go away on business for a week then..."

"It's all right, Dad," said Patrick, hurrying forward. "This is Todd. He's a friend. He's staying in the hotel too."

Roland grunted. "Hmmm. Good. That'll be someone to keep you occupied then, won't it?" He turned and went back into the room. Patrick looked really uncomfortable after his dad had said all that stuff, but I didn't have time for that right now.

"I need your help!" I said. "My sister has run off and I think she's probably gone to try and find Scout. Do you remember where room forty-two is? With the red rope and the sign saying strictly no entry?"

Patrick smiled and wiggled his eyebrows.

"No problem. I'm a human satnav!" He turned back. "I'm just going out for a bit, Dad!" he yelled. And then he stepped out and closed the door behind him.

Patrick began walking at speed and I had to almost jog to keep up with him.

"I've spent a lot of time in hotels with my dad," he

said as he walked. "Not as grim as this one, though. The hotels we usually stay in are five star and with much better signage than this one, but I've learned to look out for my own signposts so that I can get around on my own. You know what I mean?"

We came to the end of a corridor and he took a right up some stairs without any hesitation. I followed him up and up and then out on to a corridor. We came to the end and he stopped.

"Do you know which way to go now?" he said, staring at me. I looked left and right. It all looked identical to me. I had no idea. And I still didn't know what floor I was on.

"Um ... right?" I said.

"Wrong!" said Patrick. "Look, there's a fire extinguisher over there on the wall. So, it's left."

He marched on. He was so annoying but I didn't have any choice but to keep following him. Laurie could be anywhere! We walked past two rusty tin buckets. I looked up and saw that there was a big brown stain on the cracked ceiling where water had been leaking through.

"Oh, and sorry about my dad just then," said Patrick, slowing down slightly. "When he's under a lot of stress he just goes off on one sometimes.

It's work that makes him like that, you know? You shouldn't take *any* of it personally."

I wasn't so sure that any of what his dad had said was aimed at me. It was Patrick he was talking about. He had made it sound like his son was an inconvenience to him. But I didn't think it would have been nice to point that out.

"That's all right," I said.

"You can't take anything in business personally. Dad says if you get too emotional then the big fish will come along and gobble you up and then where would you be, eh?" said Patrick.

"In a big fish's belly?" I said, hoping he'd just stop talking, but Patrick looked thrilled.

"*Exactly*," said Patrick. "And there are no deals to be made in a fish's guts, are there?"

I was struggling to understand what exactly it was he was trying to say when I heard a voice I recognized.

"... and what do you think is in there? Some kind of treasure?"

We turned another corner and saw Laurie standing by the red rope. She was with Scout.

"See?" said Patrick. "Human satnav." He tapped the side of his forehead and grinned. I was more surprised that Laurie had also found where to go.

"Laurie!" I said. I was surprised how relieved I was to see her. I put my hand on her shoulder. "Don't you ever run off like that again, do you hear me? You could have got lost!"

"You called my fossils stupid, but *you* are the stupid one!" she said. "You don't want to be on holiday and that is more stupid than anything! You are the meanest brother ever."

Patrick and Scout both turned to me, waiting to see what I was going to say.

"I didn't mean it about your fossils," I said. "I'm sorry."

Laurie glared at me through her thick blonde fringe.

"Well, this is all just lovely you having a little family crisis right now, but I've only got a limited amount of time before Mum realizes that this is missing," said Scout. She held up a hotel key and jiggled it in front of us. It had the number forty-two etched on to the wooden fob.

"I don't get it," said Patrick. "What's so important about that room? And why is it shut off?"

Scout looked up and down the corridor, then stepped over the rope.

"Come down here out of sight and I'll explain," said Scout.

Patrick and I climbed over the rope and Laurie ducked underneath it as she was so small. The hotel wasn't exactly well lit, but it was even darker in the little side corridor. Not one wall light was working.

We walked along the narrow corridor, which had doors either side and one at the end all on its own. Scout stopped by this door and turned to face us.

"Imagine it's the twenty-ninth of May, 1955," began Scout. "The Paradise Hotel is full to capacity. Every room has happy guests and there are porters, waitresses, chefs and hotel managers ready to attend to anyone's needs."

"Er. No. Sorry. I can't imagine it," said Patrick, grinning to himself. Scout ignored him.

"Each evening, the guests enjoy a four-course meal cooked by some of the best chefs in the country. Then there's live music and dancing until midnight," said Scout.

Laurie wiggled. "Oh, dancing!" she said.

"The chandeliers would have been sparkling, the shiny dance floor packed with guests and everyone would have been so thrilled to be here." Scout smiled to herself as if she were imagining the scene. It must be tough knowing how little the guests thought of the Paradise Hotel now. I thought back to that older couple who walked out yesterday. They had probably remembered it as Scout had described it, when it was a glamorous place to stay.

"Back then, in 1955, the Paradise Hotel was owned by my great-great-grandmother, Edwina Patterson," said Scout.

I recognized the name.

"She's the woman in the painting in the dining room!" I said. I remembered the picture with the eyes that followed you around. I was quite good at spotting things like that.

"Yes. That's her!" said Scout brightly. "She was an author and her murder-mystery novels were bestsellers! She was *really* famous and each summer she'd come to the Paradise Hotel to write."

She looked up at the hotel room door.

"I wish I could have met her. I have so many questions I would ask her about writing and how she managed to come up with ideas for so many brilliant books. I mean, how do you even start?" she said.

"Are you a writer too?" I asked. Scout stared at her boots.

"Kind of," she said. "I'm not good like my great-great-granny was, though. Anyway, Edwina Patterson loved staying at the Paradise Hotel so much that she bought it and this became her living quarters."

Scout pointed to the door that we were standing next to. In the gloomy light I could see the door's brass handle and a little plaque which said "Room forty-two".

"Like the werewolf!" said Laurie. "He lives in the hotel too!"

Scout nodded. "She liked this room as it was very quiet and secluded and the perfect place to write her novels in peace."

I looked back at the rope that we had climbed over. She was right. This room really was hidden away.

"She lived here very happily into her old age, paying for someone to manage and run the hotel while she sat and wrote her books and looked out to sea. But then ... something happened," said Scout. "Something that has baffled people for many, many years." She paused. We were so quiet as we waited for Scout to continue that I heard Patrick swallow.

"On the twenty-ninth of May, 1955," said Scout, "Edwina Patterson disappeared."

CHAPTER SIXTEEN

"Did the werewolf eat her?"

"What do you mean she disappeared?" said Patrick. "Where'd she go?"

I felt a cold breeze on the tops of my arms and I shivered.

"Did the werewolf eat her?" whispered Laurie.

"Laurie!" I said. "There *is* no werewolf!"

"But how do you know for sure?" said Patrick. "He did look kind of wolfish."

Scout had a smile on her face as she watched the three of us. Her eyes twinkled in the darkness and she held up her hands and continued with her story.

"On the night of her disappearance she behaved exactly as she usually did. She ate her dinner in the restaurant with a small glass of white wine, then she sat and listened to the band and watched the guests dancing. At approximately nine fifteen p.m. she retired to her room and then at ten p.m. a hotel porter delivered a mug of hot cocoa to her room, which he did every evening. Edwina Patterson kept a strict routine and she would always breakfast at seven forty-five a.m., but the next morning there was no sign of her. At nine a.m. the manager was starting to get worried."

"Did the manager look for her?" asked Laurie.

"Yes. She came to her room but when she got here, the door was locked from the inside. The manager used this exact key to open it." Scout held up the gold key.

"And was she dead? In her bed?" said Laurie. "Did she die in her sleep?"

"It wouldn't be a disappearance then, would it?" said Patrick. "Let her finish!" He was clearly interested in what she had to say next. And so was I. This was all quite intriguing.

Scout began again.

"The manager opened the door and everything was as it should be. There was no sign of a disturbance. The windows were shut, her personal things were still here, but there was no sign of Edwina Patterson. My great-great-grandmother was never seen again," she said.

We were silent. I looked at the key in her hand.

"And you're trying to find out what happened after all this time?" I asked. Scout nodded.

"Yes. There are things in that room that are just . . . strange," she said. "I think. . ." She paused as if she wasn't sure whether to tell us or not. "I think there's something in this room that might help save the hotel."

She blurted it out really quickly, as if she didn't quite believe it herself. Unlike the werewolf story, it didn't feel like she was making this one up.

"And?" said Patrick. "What are you expecting to find?"

Scout folded her arms.

"I thought this *dump* was out of your comfort zone and you were off to somewhere more exotic?" she said.

Patrick shifted on his feet.

"Um, no. We're not leaving, actually," he

mumbled. "Dad has got to stay because he has a lot of meetings in the area. This is the only place that has rooms. Which isn't surprising really. You know. Considering." Scout glared at him, then turned to me.

"And what about you?" she said. "I thought you couldn't wait to leave too."

Laurie started jumping up and down.

"We are staying!" she said. "Todd didn't mean anything, did you, Todd? Please can you open the door? I want to see if there is a skeleton in there!"

"We're staying. For now," I said. I wanted to have a look inside the mystery room too. Scout nodded.

"OK," she said. "Let's go in, shall we?"

Scout stood forward and pushed the key in the lock, then slowly turned it. We heard a click. She twisted the handle and the three of us stepped inside.

The room was very dark and the windows were covered with long, heavy-looking curtains. Scout walked over and yanked them open. A cloud of dust shimmered in the sunlight coming through the window. I went over and looked outside. We were in the top corner of the hotel under one of the turrets. The view out on to the sea from this height was pretty impressive. The room was as large as our room and Dad's put together and the furniture looked antique.

There was a large four-poster bed, a bedside table, a big dark-wood wardrobe and a desk with a black typewriter. On the wall was an old clock and at the end of the bed was a large trunk with a silver padlock. I went over to take a look at the clock. It had a white face and a long bronze-coloured pendulum. The pendulum was still and the clock wasn't ticking. The time on the clock said half past ten. At the top of the clock face was a little cut-out area which showed a painting of the moon with a slice of it missing in darkness. Underneath the moon there were some swirly letters that said *First Quarter*.

"Look!" said Patrick. "It's her cocoa mug from the night she disappeared!" He picked it up. "It might contain vital evidence! Urgh. If you think brown gunk is important." He put the mug back down.

I was puzzled. How could anyone disappear from inside a locked room? It made no sense.

"If she'd disappeared then the police would have been involved. This would have been a crime scene, wouldn't it?" I said. "They would have found anything suspicious, surely?"

"Not necessarily," said Scout. "Remember, this was a long time ago and they could have easily missed something. There was a lot of interest in the case at the beginning. Newspapers had headlines like 'Bestselling Mystery Author Goes Missing'. But after a while, Edwina's disappearance was forgotten. The police had nothing to go on and life moved on."

Scout looked around the room, taking it all in.

"This room was locked up and kept exactly as it is now. Frozen in time."

Laurie was pulling on the wardrobe door, making it rattle.

"This is locked," she said. "Do you think her guts are in there?"

"Laurie! Come away," I said.

Patrick was pacing around like he was some kind of detective in an old movie.

"So, what makes you think that this room can help your hotel?" asked Patrick.

I was wondering the same thing.

"Have you found something in here?" I said.

Scout reached into her coat pocket and took out a folded piece of paper.

"Not in here, exactly," she said. "My granny was a little girl when her grandmother disappeared. But a few months after the police investigation was closed, Granny got a mysterious note addressed to her in the post," said Scout. "She died a few years back but she

139

always used to talk about it with me."

"And is that it? Is that the note?" said Patrick.

"Yes," said Scout, opening the paper. "It says, 'Room forty-two is not as it seems.'"

"Can I take a look?" I said. Scout passed the note to me and I read it myself. I checked the back of the note but it was blank.

"Who sent it?" said Patrick.

Scout took the piece of paper back, frowning. "Granny never found out. Her mum just dismissed it as some kind of prank from an old fan, but Granny always used to talk to me about it, telling me that she thought that there was something hidden in here. My mum isn't interested. She's got enough on her plate with running the hotel and she also thought it was some kind of joke, but there *is* something in this room somewhere. I just know it. And I *know* that whatever it is it will help to save the Paradise Hotel."

I looked around room forty-two. It just looked like an old-fashioned, untouched, very dusty hotel room to me.

"Why isn't this room used?" I asked Scout. "Is it like some kind of memorial to your great-great-grandmother?"

Scout shook her head.

"Not exactly," she said. "I'm not sure if you've noticed, but we are kind of a bit behind with the repairs around here."

"Huh. You're telling me!" said Patrick. "Even the roof is falling down. Dad said that will cost so much to repair it'll make your eyes water! *Tens of thousands* he reckons!"

Scout gazed down at the shabby carpet and seemed embarrassed. Patrick looked at me and bit on his bottom lip. For once he seemed to realize that he'd possibly been a little tactless.

"Has anyone stayed in here since she went missing?" I said.

"No," said Scout. "Lots of areas of the hotel have been closed off to save money on the heating and electricity. We don't have the guests to fill them, anyway. The fifth floor is completely shut. No one has stayed in any of these rooms for years. Apparently, Edwina's room was kept as it was for a while but then, as time went on and fewer and fewer guests came to stay, it was just forgotten about, I guess."

"Hang on though," said Patrick. "If you and your mum are the descendants of this Edwina, you'll have inherited her millions, surely!"

Scout frowned. "It wasn't exactly millions," she

said. "She was really famous back then, but all the money that was inherited by my great-grandmother and then my granny has been ploughed back into the hotel, trying to keep it going. By the time Mum took over, all the money was long gone. She still gets a small amount each year from the publisher for any book sales, but it's usually just enough to mend something small. Not big things like a roof, for example." She stared at Patrick, who seemed to shrink a little into his button-down shirt.

Laurie suddenly dropped down on to her knees beside the bed. She had spotted something on the floor.

"Look! Her shoes are still here!" she said. She pulled out a brown, shiny shoe which had a little black heel.

"Laurie! Don't touch that," I said. I didn't like the thought of her touching the shoes of some dead woman.

Laurie went to put the shoe back but a piece of folded paper fell out of it. She picked it up.

"There was something inside the shoe!" she gasped. She was just about to open it up when Scout sprang around.

"Sshhh!" she said. "Someone's coming!"

We all froze and listened. There was a mumbling sound outside the door. Scout looked panicked and began to look around the room but there was nowhere to hide. We were trapped.

"It's . . . it's the werewolf!" squeaked Patrick. "He's coming to get me, isn't he? For knocking on his door and disturbing him!"

"Quick! Under the bed!" said Scout.

Patrick was the first to get under, followed by me, Laurie and Scout.

The four of us lay on our stomachs like sardines squashed in a can. My face was right next to Edwina Patterson's shoe. I was so close to it I could smell the leather. The other shoe was lying on the carpet by the bedside table. Beside it was the piece of paper. Laurie must have dropped it. Patrick wriggled his arm free and reached for it just as the door to room forty-two slowly opened. Laurie squeaked next to me as Patrick's hand disappeared beneath the bed, just as two pairs of feet walked into the room.

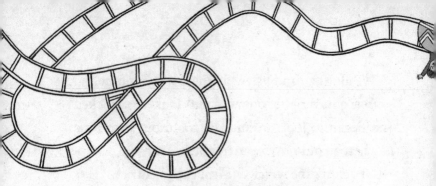

CHAPTER SEVENTEEN

"It's just a shoe."

"Oh yes, this is more like it," said a man's voice. "This room has really kept its period detail." The voice had a nasally whine to it, like a wasp trapped in a jam jar. I recognized it straight away. It was Howard Knife.

"It's been closed off for many years," said a much softer voice. It was Scout's mum, Marianne. "In fact, this room has been completely untouched since the late 1950s, I'd say."

We watched Howard's shoes as he paced around. I bit on my lip as he got so close I could make out my reflection in the shiny black leather.

"But the room was unlocked just now," said Howard. "Why would that be? Isn't that a bit ... careless of you?"

I heard Scout whimper and we all froze, waiting to see if anyone had heard her.

"I'm not sure why it's unlocked," said Marianne. "The key has been misplaced, it seems. I brought a master key with me but ... well, as you can see, it's all as it was."

Howard began to walk around.

"I'm assuming you know the story behind this room?" said Marianne.

"I had heard something about a guest disappearing?" said Howard.

"It wasn't a guest. It was my great-grandmother," said Marianne. "She actually owned the hotel at the time and—"

"A disappearing old lady is of no interest to me," Howard cut in. "It's this original decor I'm interested in. The rest of the hotel must have been updated in the 1970s, but this room looks like it dates back to the early twentieth century." He walked around.

"Obviously my offer for the Paradise Hotel is inclusive of *all* the furniture and fixtures," he said. As he moved around the room he stopped to pull on a locked drawer of the desk and then he bent down to wiggle the padlock on the trunk. It was almost as if he was looking for something.

"Of course," said Marianne, standing in one position.

"I can see this lot making a tidy sum once it's ripped out," said Howard, heading towards the door. "I'm going to have to recoup some of my investment *before* the demolition team move in."

Scout took another sharp intake of breath. I watched as Marianne's white lace-up pumps moved towards Howard.

"You are forgetting that I haven't made my final decision, Mr Knife. My family have a great deal of history in this hotel. Any decision has to be made with much care and consideration," she said.

Howard Knife took another step towards the door.

"Of course, Ms Patterson. I know you see me as some kind of villain, but can I assure you that..." Howard Knife suddenly stopped talking. He walked towards the bed, then crouched down and picked up the shoe that Laurie had dropped. I held my breath. If he looked slightly to his right he'd clearly be able to see four faces hiding under the bed. He frowned as he stared at the shoe, then he turned and looked straight at us. I was expecting him to look surprised or maybe angry, but his face, as he stared, stayed rigid and showed no emotion.

"Is everything all right, Mr Knife?" said Marianne. She hadn't moved and couldn't see us from where she was standing.

Howard glared at us before getting back up.

"Everything is fine," he said. "It's just a shoe."

"How strange," said Marianne. "I wonder how that got there."

He dropped the shoe back on the floor with a thump. The four of us flinched as it landed close to Patrick's face.

"Well, Ms Patterson," said Howard. "My lawyers will draw up the contract. I estimate it'll be ready in three days."

"Three days! But I need longer than that," said Marianne with panic in her voice. "I need to weigh up all of my options and talk to the bank again and. . ."

"Options? But you don't have any options, Ms Patterson," said Howard. "Do you want the Paradise Hotel to drag you further and further into debt? You *do* know how suffocating it can be down there, don't you?"

There was silence from Marianne, but I guessed she'd nodded.

"I'll show you the way out," she said. We watched the door open and Marianne's feet disappeared. Howard Knife paused for a moment; he was still facing our direction. Then he turned and followed, banging the door behind him.

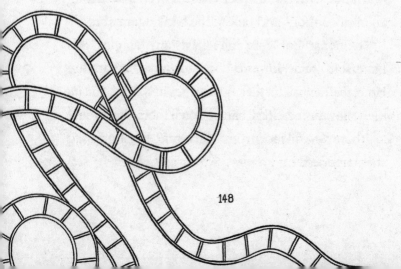

CHAPTER EIGHTEEN

"You won't be on your own this time."

We dragged ourselves out from under the bed and Scout sat down on it.

"He saw us. He *definitely* saw us, didn't he?" she said.

"Yep," I said. "I can't believe he didn't say anything."

Patrick sighed. "That's good, isn't it?" he said. "He must have other things on his mind, like knocking this place down."

Scout spun around. "He is not knocking anything down and he won't be buying the Paradise Hotel, OK?"

Patrick held his hands up. "All right, all right," he

149

said. "I'm just repeating what I heard! But it's clear this place is destined to be rubble."

"Patrick!" I said. He looked at me blankly.

"It doesn't make sense," said Scout. "Howard Knife detests me and if he thought he could get me into trouble he would have. But he didn't say a thing!"

It did seem strange, but then he probably thought we were just kids, messing around. I thought back to what he'd said to Marianne, about all their debts.

"It sounds like your mum doesn't really have much of a choice about selling the hotel, does she?" I said. "Not if she's got ... money issues."

Scout didn't say anything. She just sat there, staring at the floor. She suddenly seemed smaller and all of her boldness had melted away. I looked at Patrick. He was pacing around the room intently and chewing on the side of his thumb. Laurie had picked up the shoe that Howard had dropped. She knelt down by the bed and put it back, next to the other one.

"I know you don't want to leave here but at least it'll mean that your mum won't have to worry any more. And that's something, isn't it?" I said. "Worrying is horrible."

Scout looked at me with fear in her eyes. "Three

days, Todd," she said. "I've only got three days to save my home." She walked away and stood by the window.

I didn't know what to say to make her feel better.

Patrick came over to me with something in his hand. It was the piece of paper that had fallen out of the shoe.

"What is it, Patrick?" I said.

He unfolded it. There was one word written in the centre of the paper.

Moon

"Moon," read Laurie. "Why would that be hidden in a shoe?"

Patrick picked up one of the shoes and inspected it, shaking it to see if anything else would fall out. Then he did the same to the other shoe. They were both empty.

"Hmmm," said Patrick. He looked again at the piece of paper. "This is very interesting."

"Could it be a clue?" said Scout, rushing over. "The note that my great-grandma received said that the room was not as it seems. Maybe this means something?"

I thought Scout was sounding a bit desperate.

"It's probably just the make of the shoe," I said. "Like a brand name or something."

But Scout took out the other piece of paper that said about the room not being as it seemed.

"Look!" she said excitedly. "It's the same handwriting!"

She held it up. "Whoever sent the message to Great-Granny saying that the room wasn't as it seems also hid this note saying moon!"

They did look very similar, but I was puzzled. "But why hide notes?" I said. "What is the point and what does it mean?" I noticed that Patrick had a slight smile on his lips.

"I think we should hang on to the note. It might be important," he said. And he tucked the slip of paper into his jeans pocket. There was suddenly a loud crackling sound and a voice came from Scout's coat.

"MUM TO SCOUT. WHERE ARE YOU? I'VE JUST GOT TO THE KITCHEN AND YOU'RE NOT HERE! WE NEED TO GET LUNCH READY. OVER."

Scout took the walkie-talkie out of her pocket.

"COMING. OVER," she said. Her shoulders slumped.

"I've got to go," she said. "Mum needs me."

We all headed to the door, but Patrick was standing staring at the clock.

"Patrick? Are you coming?" I said. He stood there for a moment, then followed us. We went outside and Scout put the key in the door and locked it. We headed down the narrow hallway and Scout, Patrick and I stepped over the rope. Laurie ducked underneath it again.

"I wish there was something we could do to help you, Scout," said Laurie. "I know! I could sell my collection of precious fossils! Then you and your mum can keep living here. And the werewolf can stay too!"

"Don't be stupid, Laurie," I muttered. Scout scowled at me, then turned to my sister.

"That's really kind of you, Laurie," she said. "Thank you. But I think we need a lot more money than you realize."

Patrick was quiet as we walked. "Hey," he said, "did anyone else think room forty-two felt a bit like an ... escape room?"

"An escape room?" said Scout. "What's an escape room?"

I was glad she asked because I didn't know what one was either. And I wasn't sure if it was something that I should know about.

"Have you never been to one? They're brilliant," said Patrick. "You go into a room and you have to solve lots of puzzles to get out. It's like a game. Me and my friends go all the time."

"And you're locked in the room? Like you're in prison?" said Laurie.

Patrick laughed.

"Kind of. But it's fun! There are all these objects and mysterious things hidden in strange places. You work as a team and the aim is to solve all of the clues. There's a time limit and you need to solve the room within that time."

"But what if you can't?" said Laurie. "Do you get locked in for ever?"

"Of course not! It just means you didn't win, that's all," said Patrick. "I did one with my mates for my birthday. All escape rooms have some kind of theme and the one we did was like an old-fashioned bank with a vault and everything! And we had to solve who had robbed it. It was like walking into a crime scene. It was brilliant! We solved the room in fifty-seven minutes and seven seconds."

We turned a corner.

"I don't understand what that has to do with room forty-two though," I said.

Patrick chewed his lip.

"Yeah, it's probably hard to understand if you haven't done one before," he said. But he didn't say it in a mean way like Joe might have. They would have made me feel like I was stupid for not knowing what an escape room was. Patrick carried on.

"To me, it felt like room forty-two was all set up, waiting to be solved. The objects felt like props: the typewriter, the cocoa mug, the stopped clock on the wall. Then there was the locked wardrobe and that padlocked trunk. That's another thing about escape rooms – you always have things to unlock."

As he spoke he became more excited by the idea. I looked at Scout, who was silent and clearly thinking about what he was suggesting.

"So, you're saying that room forty-two is ... an escape room?" she said. The lights on the corridor walls flickered like flames on a candle.

"Not exactly. I'm sure they didn't exist in 1955, for a start. What I'm saying is that I think the room is like a big puzzle. And I think whoever murdered Edwina Patterson has left a trail of clues, ready to be solved."

"MURDERED!" shouted Laurie. "HAS SHE BEEN MURDERED?"

"Sshhhh, Laurie!" I said. "Of course she hasn't been murdered. Has she, Scout?" I certainly didn't fancy suddenly finding a body.

Scout shrugged. "Who knows," she said. "There *was* a werewolf living here at the time."

I did some maths. "But if the werewolf was living here all that time ago, doesn't that make him like a hundred and fifty years old or something?" I said.

Scout nodded. "Yes, I guess it does," she said, as if that was the most normal thing in the world.

"Well, I think we should go back to room forty-two and investigate properly," said Patrick.

Scout folded her arms. "I thought you and your dad hated this place?" she said.

Patrick laughed nervously.

"I guess it sounds like that," he said, "but to be honest, I've been to many hotels with Dad and it always ends up the same. Dad complains a lot, then sits in the room working while I end up wandering around on my own. It can be a bit boring, to be honest. Even in the best hotels with the nicest swimming pools."

It sounded quite lonely and not much fun at all.

"This is going to be a nice holiday for you, isn't it, Patrick?" said Laurie. "You won't be on your own this time." Patrick glanced sideways at my little sister.

"What do you mean?" he said.

She thought about it for a bit. "Well, you said that usually your daddy is busy working so you're on your own. But on *this* holiday, you've got us! *And* you've got a thingy room to solve ... a 'Can You Escape Room'! Which you love because you said you do them all the time, didn't you?"

Patrick smiled. "Yeah, I guess I did say that, didn't I?" he said.

"And how about you, Todd?" said Scout. "You're here with your dad, aren't you? Where is he?"

"Daddy is really, *really* tired!" piped up Laurie. "He's been in bed *a lot*."

I gave her a discreet shove.

"It's only a virus," I said. "He's just resting until he feels better."

"Bummer," said Patrick.

We walked on in silence for a while and then Laurie started talking again.

"When can we go back to the room, Scout?" she said. "So we can solve the 'moon' clue!"

"How about we meet up after lunch?" said Scout. "I've got to help Mum for a bit but I can meet you afterwards?"

"Can we, Todd?" said Laurie. She grinned and looked at me with pleading eyes, but I wasn't so sure. I couldn't deny that I was intrigued. What if there really was treasure? And what had actually happened to Edwina Patterson? But the reality was that I had Dad to worry about. I was still hoping he'd be able to drive us home later.

"Let's see how Dad is feeling first, eh?" I said it quietly, even though Patrick and Scout could clearly hear.

"Well, I'll definitely be there! You'll be needing my super-intelligent brain for sure," said Patrick. He grinned and tapped his forehead. "There's a lot of grey matter in here, you know."

Laurie grabbed me on my arm.

"Please can we go, Todd?" she said. "PLEASE!"

If we'd been on our own I would probably have told her to be quiet and stop acting like a baby, but Patrick and Scout were both staring at me. I sighed. I guessed it would be late afternoon before Dad was ready to drive anyway.

"OK," I said. "But just for a little while."

"Yes!" said Laurie, clapping her hands together.

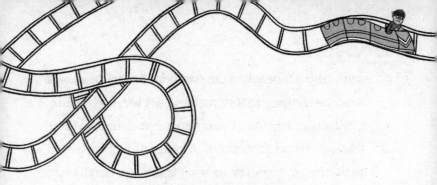

CHAPTER NINETEEN

"I'll organize everything."

Laurie and I headed back to our room, her wittering all the way about hidden treasure and murdered authors. As we got closer to room twenty-three, I crossed my fingers, hoping that Dad would be up. But when we opened the door, everything was the same: the same musty smell and Dad still in bed.

"Shall I open a window, Dad?" I said as we walked in.

He didn't answer. His face was hidden underneath the sheet.

Laurie stood at the bottom of his bed and stared at

him. I think for the first time since we'd got here, she was actually realizing that he really wasn't very well at all.

"Laurie, why don't you go and sort through your fossils?" I said. "Put them in order of your favourite to your least favourite or something like that?"

Laurie thought about it for a moment and then she headed into our room. I heard the familiar rattle of her plastic tub being tipped out.

I went over to the curtains and opened them. The window was one of those box-shaped ones where you have to lift it up to open it. It was raining again, but only lightly. I pushed on the window frame but it only budged a few centimetres. I guessed it was better than nothing. I picked up the mug of cold coffee and the glass of water from Dad's bedside table and poured them down the sink in the bathroom. I refilled the glass with fresh water and put it back on his bedside table. None of the food had been touched. I sat down on the bed and Dad stirred.

"Dad?" I said. "You've got to eat something. How about a banana? That'll make you feel better, don't you think?"

I waited, then picked up the banana and began to peel it.

"Dad?" I said again. "Please eat something."

Moving as if in slow motion, Dad turned over. He looked up at me. His eyes had dark shadows under them and when he blinked it looked like his eyelids were almost too heavy to lift.

"Here, eat this," I said. I held the banana towards him. He stared at it as if he wasn't actually sure what it was, then, very slowly, he raised himself up on to his elbow. I held the banana closer to his lips and he took a small bite. I could feel my throat tightening and my head began to pound. As I watched my father swallowing the piece of banana, I wanted to cry and tell him that he had to get better, *right now*. But instead, I chewed on the side of my cheek to stop the tears. Dad took another bite, then reached to hold the banana himself. His hand squeezed mine as he took it.

"There you go," I said. "You'll feel better after eating." I picked up the glass of water.

"Have a drink too," I said.

Dad leaned forward and I held the glass to his lips so that he could take a sip.

"Thank you, Todd," he whispered. I noticed that the corners of his eyes were damp. I really, really didn't want to see my dad crying. What was wrong with him? Why was he being like this? I looked away and pretended that I hadn't noticed. There was an old-looking alarm clock on the bedside table that had a radio built in.

"Shall I put some music on for you while you're resting?" I said. He nodded, very slowly, before taking another small bite of the banana. Then he put the banana beside his glass and lay back down. He hadn't eaten much at all.

I knelt by the radio and worked out how to put it on. The dial lit up and a woman was talking about the benefits of gardening for your mental health.

"... and when we are outside in the fresh air we can focus on the small details of nature around us..."

I twiddled the knob to try and find a station that was playing music. I tuned past one playing rap and another playing classical music and tried to find something Dad would like. Maybe listening to happy songs would help to make him feel better?

The sound of a woman's singing voice caught my attention and I stopped and tuned the radio as best I could. I knew the song – it was one of Mum's favourites. The woman had a really powerful voice and she was singing about how she wanted to dance with somebody who loved her. I looked at Dad as he lay back on his pillow with his eyes shut. There was a small smile on his lips. I wondered if he was remembering what had popped into my head as soon as I'd heard it. Mum's fortieth birthday party...

The party was about a year before Mum and Dad split up and before she was offered the job where she had to live abroad for months at a time. Her birthday was in July and she told Dad that she didn't want any fuss, but Dad said it was too big a birthday to let it go past without having a proper celebration.

"Leave it to me, Alison," said Dad to Mum. "I'll organize *everything*." And he did. He sent invitations to around fifty friends and family. I remember thinking that there was no way on earth that all those people would fit into our house, but he borrowed a gazebo from Aunt Lexie's friend Kim which filled our entire garden like a giant extra room. He decorated the gazebo with some tube lighting that flashed with multicoloured dots of light and put up a big pinboard filled with photographs of Mum as a little girl and pictures of me and Laurie with her when we were babies. I was ten at the time and Laurie was four and both of us were so excited. I remember running around the big, empty gazebo before the guests arrived. Dad's friend Duncan was in charge of the barbecue and Duncan's girlfriend, Kelly, was sorting the music. She was a professional DJ and she'd planned the whole playlist using Mum's favourite songs.

The party was a huge success and Laurie and I were both allowed to stay up right until the end, but by eleven p.m. I was getting really tired. I sat on a chair on the edge of the gazebo and my back felt sweaty against the plastic. I watched the adults dancing and laughing around me. Mum was standing by the entrance to the gazebo, smiling and chatting to a group of people I didn't know. Over the speakers a woman's voice quivered and whooped and began to sing a song about a clock striking the hour. Mum suddenly whooped and ran away from the people she was chatting to and towards me. At first, I thought she was going to try and get me to dance, but instead she kicked off her shoes under my chair, gave me a kiss on the top of my head, then ran to the middle of the dance floor. Dad appeared from another corner and swept her up into a hug, spinning her round and round as the music played. He put her down and the two of them danced and grinned and sang into each other's faces. I sat on that plastic chair and I watched as the coloured lights danced on Mum's blonde, shiny hair, and I remember thinking I'd probably never seen a happier couple in my whole life.

The song on the radio in room twenty-three came to an end and the presenter began talking. I looked at Dad and the smile on his face had gone.

"Dad?" I said. "I think … I think that maybe you are feeling like this because you stopped taking those tablets in the bathroom cabinet. Don't you? They're still there at home. I was going to bring them with me but … but I didn't. I didn't think I should touch them. Do you think that's the reason you feel so sad?"

I waited and watched his face. I hoped that his eyes would flicker open and he'd agree with me. He'd say that yes, that's why he was feeling bad and all he had to do was to start taking them again. Then he'd be better.

But he didn't reply. Dad had fallen asleep once more.

CHAPTER TWENTY

"Are werewolves smart?"

Laurie and I made our way to the dining room to get some lunch, even though I wasn't hungry. My stomach was too churned up from worrying about Dad.

The dining room was set out like it had been for breakfast, but this time the side table was filled with platters of sandwiches, crusty bread and a big pot full of tomato soup. We were the only guests in the dining room and Laurie ran over and began to pile a plate high with sandwiches. I ladled a spoonful of soup into a bowl and took Laurie to a table. As there was no one around, I thought it would be a good time to get some more food for Dad. I went back and chose some sandwiches for him, wrapping them in a napkin before stuffing them into my hoodie pocket.

Laurie and I sat down to eat just as Patrick came in with his dad. His dad looked at the food and shook his head.

"As I suspected. A feeble excuse," he said. He picked up a perfectly OK-looking sandwich and dropped it again. "No. This is no good. Come on, Patrick. Let's get out of this dump and get a decent lunch from somewhere."

I didn't think the lunch looked bad at all. There wasn't a huge selection, but it was all homemade and had been set out nicely. Scout and her mum were doing a pretty good job considering it was just the two of them.

Roland Harris turned to go, but Patrick looked over at us.

"Can I stay here, Dad?" said Patrick. "I can meet you back in the suite later?"

Patrick's dad looked a little confused but then waved his hand.

"Yes. Yes, whatever," he said. "No earlier than four p.m. though, remember? I've got a conference call at three."

Patrick's head dropped as his dad walked out of the dining room. Then he helped himself to some food and rushed over to our table.

"Hi!" he said. He stuffed a triangle of tuna sandwich in his mouth. "Have you seen Scout yet?"

"She's over there!" said Laurie. "Scout! Scout!"

Scout was just walking into the dining room carrying a tray of cakes. She was wearing a white top and black trousers. It was the first time I'd see her without her long heavy coat. She looked a lot smaller without it. It was almost like the coat and the goggles were some kind of costume, or armour. She put the cakes down and headed over.

She stood by our table, looking really miserable. Patrick wriggled in his seat.

"I've been looking on the internet about the disappearance of Edwina Patterson," he said. "You're right, the police were involved and there were no conclusions drawn about what happened to her, but I was thinking, they probably weren't looking in the right kind of places, were they?"

"What do you mean?" said Scout, perking up.

"They were looking for evidence of something to lead them to Edwina Patterson: like a handwritten letter, or fingerprints, or traces of blood. If they'd found the note saying 'moon' in her shoe, then so what? They would have dismissed it as nothing," he said. "There was nothing to lead them to a crime."

"So there *is* no crime then?" I said. I was confused about what Patrick was telling us. "She wasn't murdered?"

Patrick shrugged.

"Or whoever is behind her disappearance is some kind of criminal genius and wants to show off how clever they are," he said.

"Are werewolves clever?" asked Laurie, working her way through a fourth sandwich.

Scout sat down. "Of course!" she said. "The thing about werewolves is that they are like two different people in one. One person is calm and just like any one of us, but when there is a full moon ... BAM! *That's* when they change. *That's* when the quiet, calm person just goes *wild*."

"Like Daddy!" said Laurie, grinning. "He can be all quiet and tired, then, all of sudden, BAM! He goes crazy!"

I glared at her and there was an awkward silence. I looked at Patrick and Scout, but they were both acting like they hadn't heard anything, although they clearly had. I carried on eating.

We sat there for a bit and then Patrick reached into his pocket and pulled out the folded piece of paper that had fallen out of Edwina Patterson's shoe.

"I was thinking about this piece of paper and it definitely looks like a clue," he said. He unfolded it and we all stared at the writing:

Moon

"There's something in that room that is going to make sense of this little note, I just know it," said Patrick. "You need to get us back into that room, Scout. I'm an escape room expert – I can help!"

Scout stared at the paper, a small smile on her face. She looked happier than she had done a minute ago.

"Agreed," she said. "Let's meet there in an hour."

We all nodded. I stood up and Dad's parcel of sandwiches fell out of my hoodie's pocket into a messy heap on the table. For a few blissful moments the thought of solving the puzzle of Edwina's room had made me forget all about Dad being unwell. But the worries all came flooding back. Patrick and Scout stared at the sandwiches and then at each other.

"They're for my dad," I said. "He's still not

feeling well."

I glanced up at Patrick and Scout. They both looked like they had questions but they didn't ask them.

"Our auntie says that we live on a rollercoaster!" said Laurie brightly. "We go up and down and up and down."

"Laurie, would you just *stop* talking for once?" I said. Laurie screwed her nose up at me. I felt my cheeks beginning to burn.

Patrick shifted around awkwardly. "I'm going to go and get some soup," he said. He got up and headed over to the buffet.

"I'll get a bag for you to put the food in," said Scout. "I won't be long."

I was so embarrassed. It was becoming increasingly obvious that our dad was incapable of doing anything for us. He'd be better soon, surely? And then we could get out of here and go home.

I piled the sandwiches on to a plate and when Scout came back I grabbed the paper bag from her.

"Thanks," I said. Scout just stood there, watching me.

"Does anyone know your dad isn't well?" she said gently. "How about your mum? Have you called her? Shouldn't you call a doctor or something?"

"I don't want to talk about it," I snapped.

Some guests came in and headed to a table in the corner and then Marianne appeared at the kitchen door.

"Scout!" she called. "Can you come and help, please?" Scout walked off and the door to the kitchen swung back and forth from the force of being pushed. Laurie tugged on my sleeve.

"Todd? Can we go to the beach while we wait for Scout?" she said. "So I can find some more fossils?" I shook her hand off and ignored her as I put the sandwiches into the paper bag.

"Todd? Please? Please can we go to the beach?" said Laurie, putting on her really desperate voice.

"Laurie, just stop it, OK?" I said, glaring at her.

She sighed and we headed out of the restaurant. We had only reached the stairs in reception before she started up again.

"Please can we go to the beach, Todd? *Please!*" she said. "You promised!"

"Laurie, I did no such thing," I said. "And Dad isn't well enough to go, OK? Stop being such a pain!"

Her face scrunched up and she started to cry.

Great. That was all I needed. I stomped off up the stairs and I could hear her sniffling as she followed me.

Back at our room, Dad was propped up on his pillow with his eyes closed. The radio was still on but he must have turned it down. I could barely hear it. Laurie ran into our room and I heard a squeak followed by muffled sobbing as she threw herself on to her bed. I ignored her and stood beside Dad's bed.

"Hi, Dad," I said. "I brought you some lunch."

His eyes opened and he smiled at me. "Thank you, Todd," he said. I put the paper bag on the bed beside him. "Is Laurie OK?" said Dad. "How are you doing?"

"Laurie's fine. She's just got the hump about not going to the beach, that's all," I said. Dad stared down at the bedcovers, frowning. I didn't think he was really listening.

"You should probably eat something, Dad," I said. I thought about what Scout had said. "And maybe you should call a doctor? Or . . . or I can tell Mum?"

"No. No doctors," said Dad. "And there's no need to worry your mum. I'll be fine soon, Todd. Honestly. And anyway, you're like my doctor, aren't you? Look, I'm going to eat something, just like you told me to."

He took a sandwich out of the paper bag and began to nibble it. Seeing him sitting up and eating a bit more made me feel a little better. His jaw was moving really slowly, like the sandwich was made of glue rather than bread and ham. The effort of talking and eating seemed to be wearing him out again and he closed his eyes while he chewed.

I went into our room and Laurie's sobbing instantly went up a decibel, which I knew was only because she had an audience. I ignored her. If she wanted to have a full-blown tantrum when she didn't get her own way, then that was *her* problem. Not mine. I went into the bathroom and locked the door. I ran the tap and splashed water on to my face, then stared in the mirror. I had dark shadows under my eyes and somehow I looked older. My phone vibrated in my back pocket. I took it out and groaned when I saw that there was a message waiting for me in the group chat.

Blake: THIS is how to holiday, Todd!

Underneath was a photo of Blake and Joe both wearing sunglasses and sitting in kayaks. I knew where the photo was taken – it was on a water-sports lake not far from where we lived. I'd never been but I think Joe had sailing lessons there. They looked so happy against the blue sky. Joe had his hand shading his eyes from the sun. The weather was clearly *way* better back home too. I swallowed and quickly typed a one-word answer that didn't give away how gutted I was feeling.

Todd: Brilliant!

Blake was typing another message and I waited to see what he was about to say.

Blake: You should come next time! Do you remember when we went on paddleboards after we finished primary school?!

I did remember! His mum had taken us for an end-of-term treat. We had laughed so much that day. Especially when Blake couldn't keep his balance and kept falling in. I was just about to reply about how much fun it had been when a message popped up from Joe.

Joe: Panic Button? On a Paddle Board?
MATCH MADE IN HEAVEN!

My heart sank. I could feel my friendship with Blake edging further and further away. Who would I hang around with if he was with Joe all the time? And it was clear that Joe really didn't like me at all.

I was just thinking of what to text back when I heard the sound of a door banging. I went out of the bathroom and saw that Laurie wasn't on her bed any more.

"Laurie?" I said. I went into Dad's room.

"Dad? Have you seen Laurie?" But Dad had rolled on to his side and I could hear him snoring. The hotel room door was slightly ajar.

I huffed. Laurie had run off again. This time I was tempted to just let her go. She clearly expected me to follow her, but maybe if I didn't, she'd learn her lesson after all.

I went back in our room and then I noticed something on the floor, between our beds. It was Laurie's suitcase. It had been tipped upside down as if she'd been searching for something, and then I spotted that her anorak – that bundled up into a little purple bag – was missing. I knew she'd definitely brought it as I'd put it in her case myself. There was also no sign of her tub of fossils underneath her pillow.

The sound of rain hitting against the window made me flinch. I realized exactly where my little sister was heading to, all on her own.

The beach.

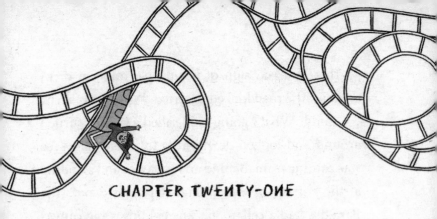

CHAPTER TWENTY-ONE

"I just want us to have a nice holiday."

I broke into a run and headed downstairs to reception. The welcome desk was empty so there was no one to ask if they'd seen Laurie heading outside.

I pushed the heavy glass door open and stepped out into the pouring rain. A car drove past, its wheels splashing rainwater into the air. I ran down the hotel steps and jumped the last two. My feet skidded as I landed on the wet pavement.

"Laurie!" I yelled down the street. I spun around. "Laurie, where are you?"

There was no sign of her purple raincoat or of anyone. The road looked deserted. Where was she?

"Todd? What's going on?" called a voice. I turned around and looked downwards to where the voice was coming from. Behind an iron fence and standing at the bottom of some metal steps was Scout. The Paradise had a cellar. She was holding a big canvas bag that had "bed linen" written on one side.

"Have you seen my sister?" I gasped.

"No. What's happened? Is everything OK?" she said.

"She's gone! She ... she just left without me realizing and ... and I think she's gone to the beach on her own!" I said. I wiped rainwater from my eyes. I was getting soaked.

Scout dropped the big bag and ran up the steps, which clanked with her heavy boots.

"Come on, we can probably catch up with her!" she said. I ran after her into the driving rain. Scout stopped for a car to pass and then headed across the road. We were right by the sea wall now and the waves were big and fierce. They thundered towards the shore and crashed on to the pebbles, throwing up white, frothy foam. I scanned the beach but I couldn't see her anywhere. Scout began to jog and I caught up and ran beside her. Just ahead was the fenced-off funfair that we had passed in the car on the day we arrived.

"The funfair has been shut down for years!" shouted Scout over the noise of the waves and the wind and rain. "Since it closed, the holidaymakers didn't seem so keen to come here." We ran along the wire fence. There was a bright red sign that said:

DANGER – KEEP OUT
TRESPASSERS WILL BE PROSECUTED

Behind the fence was a helter-skelter, its colourful paintwork now faded and flaking. On the top, a tatty flag was blowing in the wind and rain. I also spotted a dodgem ride with its little cars rusting and parked in one corner. There was a small Ferris wheel behind the dodgems and other stalls that had games or sold food. It was as if one day, everyone had just vanished and the funfair had been left frozen in time. It was still and quiet like a graveyard.

I gripped on to the fence with my fingers and

stared in. And that's when I saw it. Looming against the stormy, dark-grey sky was a tall iron rollercoaster track. The ride consisted of two loop the loops and lots of twists that soared up and plummeted down. My stomach clenched as I stared up at it. It looked utterly terrifying.

I turned back to Scout.

"Do you think she could have got in here?" I said. "She might have found a gap in the fence and—"

I stopped. There was a flash of purple on the beach behind Scout's shoulder.

"There she is!" I said. It was Laurie. She was kneeling on the stones with her head hanging down.

"Laurie!" I shouted. But my voice was snatched away in the wind and she didn't hear me.

"Laurie!" yelled Scout.

We ran down the stone steps and jumped down on to the beach, the stones shifting beneath our feet. Laurie looked so small sitting there, all alone in the pouring rain.

"Laurie! What are you doing?" I shouted. She heard me then and turned around. Her eyes were bright red and her face was wet from tears and the rain. I crouched down beside her and put my hand on her back.

"It's not safe here on your own!" I said. "What were you thinking?"

She shuddered with sobs.

"I ... I dropped them!" she wailed, sobbing even harder.

Her plastic tub of "fossils" was upturned on the beach. The stones must have scattered amongst the thousands of others.

"Oh, Laurie," I said.

She turned towards me and threw her arms around my neck. "I don't want to go home," she said, sniffling on to my shoulder. "I want to stay here. I just want us to ... to have a nice holiday."

I wrapped my arms around her and lifted her up. Scout bent down and began to select some stones, placing them in the plastic tub.

"But Dad isn't very well and—"

"But he's just *tired*," said Laurie. She lifted up her head and stared at me. Her nose was snotty. "He can stay in bed and rest and we can bring him food, just like Auntie Lexie did that time. And then we can have a nice holiday. You and me."

Scout stood up.

"Here you are, Laurie," she said, holding out the tub, which now had a small selection of stones in it. "I'm sure they're not as good as your original fossils, but they look nice, don't you think?" My sister frowned and peered into the tub, sniffing. She nodded then put the lid on top. Scout took a tissue from her pocket and helped her to wipe her face.

"Why don't we go back to the hotel and I'll make us all a nice hot chocolate," said Scout. "Does that sound good?"

Laurie's face immediately lit up and she smiled. Her hand slipped into mine and I gave it a tight squeeze.

"You must never run off like that again, OK?" I said. "You really frightened me."

"Sorry, Todd," she said.

We made our way across the wet shingle beach to the stone steps. Scout turned to face me.

"Maybe Laurie's right, you know," said Scout. "Maybe it *is* best that you stay. You know, if your dad's poorly."

We crossed the road towards the hotel. It really was a very impressive building, even with the scaffolding covering most of the front.

"I was thinking," said Scout. "If your dad just needs rest, then this is probably the best place for him, don't you think? A virus can last for a few days, you know. Or even longer. He can stay in your room

182

and sleep. I can help get him his meals and you and Laurie can have a holiday. I know it's not the Bahamas or anything. But hey, there is always the mystery of room forty-two to solve, eh? I could really do with your help and you never know, it might be fun!"

Her eyebrows were all scrunched up and her face was flushed.

"Maybe," I said. I was so tired, I didn't want to think about it any more. We walked into the reception and I brushed the rain off my jeans. I was drenched. Patrick ran over to us.

"Hi!" he said. "Everything OK? Where have you been?"

"Laurie here wanted to do a bit of sightseeing," said Scout. Laurie smiled shyly. "And Todd was just deciding if they are going to stay or not."

"Oh, right," said Patrick. "And?"

Laurie looked up at me and pulled on my arm hopefully.

"Please, Todd?" she said. "*Please?*"

Scout's forehead was knitted together as she waited to hear what I was going to say. She was right, she did need our help, like I had needed hers just now to find Laurie. This was her home and I couldn't imagine how awful it must feel to know you might lose it.

"We're staying," I said.

"Yay!" said Laurie. Scout's face relaxed and she gave me the biggest smile.

"Excellent," said Patrick. "We have an escape room team ready to go!"

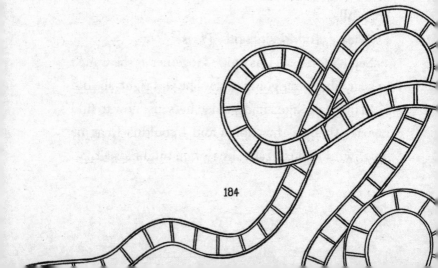

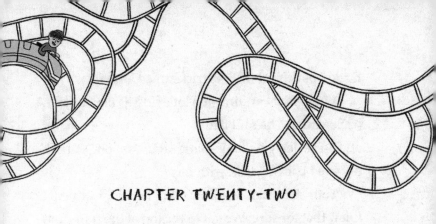

CHAPTER TWENTY-TWO

"Why is Patrick talking funny?"

Scout got the four of us some hot chocolate and we sat on the scruffy pink sofa and drank it. It was sickly sweet and delicious. Then Laurie, Patrick and I made our way to room forty-two while Scout finished sorting out the bed linen. She was going to meet us there.

Laurie held Patrick's hand, swinging it back and forth as they walked up the stairs.

"... and then I found a prehistoric shark's tooth in our rose bed, *and* a pterodactyl's claw near where

Daddy puts our bins!" Patrick stifled a yawn.

"Wow. That certainly is a lot of fossils in your own back garden," he said flatly.

Laurie let go of his hand and ran on. Patrick dropped back to walk with me.

"Your sister can certainly talk," he said. I smiled. I knew that for sure. We got to the top of the stairs and a light flickered above us.

"Urgh. That's rank," said Patrick, pointing to a particularly horrible piece of stained carpet. "This place really is in a bit of a state, isn't it?" We carried on up the stairs.

"Yep. And Scout seems to think that we are going to solve all their problems in room forty-two," I said. "Do you think there's anything in there?"

Patrick sighed. "I'm not sure. But what I do know is that Scout has a bad case of business-failure denial. Dad sees it all the time – business owners clinging on with their fingertips. And what they don't realize is they are just making it all worse for themselves by putting off the inevitable."

"What do you mean?" I said.

"I mean that the offer they've had from Howard Knife is probably the only one they'll get. If they don't take it, then . . . I don't know what will happen to them."

The wall lights in the stairwell flickered again, then died. Laurie was waiting for us at the next floor and we looked down the corridors. All the lights were off.

Patrick went over to the switch and turned it on and off again. Nothing happened. "It looks like the electricity has gone," he said.

"Maybe they haven't paid a bill and it's been switched off?" I said. That had happened to a girl in school last term. She'd told her best friend about it in confidence, but the friend had told someone else and before long we all knew. I remember Joe made a joke about it to me and Blake. Blake had laughed, but I didn't find it very funny.

We carried on walking until we got to the top floor and then we looked down the hallway into the gloom.

"This is not good," said Patrick. "There should be some kind of emergency lighting in place when there's an electricity failure. It's basic health and safety!" He took out his phone and turned on the torch. Then he led the way along the winding corridors. Eventually, I spotted the red rope across the corridor. Someone was standing behind it in the gloom. I swallowed and my heart missed a few beats. They were motionless, and I wondered if it was the werewolf, waiting to pounce on us. But then they turned on a torch and their face lit up.

"Looks like we've got a power cut." It was Scout. She'd changed out of her work gear and was back in her goggles and long coat. "It happens sometimes. Some of the wiring is a bit . . . old. It'll be back on any minute now, you wait and see."

"Hang on a sec!" said Patrick. "How did you get here before us?" Scout's eyes blinked in the torchlight.

"Aha, that would be telling," said Scout with a grin. "Right, are you ready to go back in?" She was holding the silver key in her hand. Patrick nodded. I felt a flicker of excitement deep in my stomach, even though I didn't really believe there was going to be anything in there. We climbed over the rope and Laurie ducked underneath.

Scout unlocked the door and we stepped into room forty-two again. The window let a fair amount of light in so Patrick and Scout turned their torches off. Then Patrick began to pace back and forth like he was addressing an audience.

"Right," he said "I've been thinking about this and we need to approach this in a methodical, logical manner. If we work as a team and we pull together we'll start seeing results."

Laurie tugged on my jumper. "Why is Patrick

188

talking funny?" she said. I shrugged. Patrick had clearly spent a lot of time around his dad. He carried on with his speech.

"Take a look around and tell me what things stand out to you. Anything at all. Ready? GO!"

Laurie started giggling. "A BIG BED!" she shouted.

"A bed! That's good. . . Is there anything odd about the bed?" said Patrick. We all looked at it.

"No, it looks perfectly ordinary. Apart from it being a four-poster and the pair of shoes left underneath, maybe?" said Scout.

"Yep. Those shoes were definitely significant. The note was in there so they've served their purpose," said Patrick. "And then there's the cocoa mug. That could be important but I'm not sure why. Anything else?"

"What about the clock?" I said. We all walked over to it.

"It stopped at half past ten," said Scout.

"And it is showing a picture of the moon," I said. "It says *First Quarter*."

"Yes. That's good," said Patrick. He looked around. "Doesn't this feel like the set of a play to you? Like one of those old murder mystery ones where everyone wears tweed and smokes pipes. And Edwina

Patterson is the character who has been murdered!"

"Yes!" said Scout. "Or it's a bit like one of Edwina's books and we are the characters in it!"

They were right. It did feel like this room was "staged" in some way. But maybe I was just wanting to see it like that?

"And look! There's a fish!" said Laurie. She ran over to a dark corner of the room near the wardrobe. Hanging on the wall was a small, square painting. I hadn't noticed it before. It was a painting of a fish which was reddish in colour. Its eyes bulged a bit like a cartoon fish but the rest of the painting was very detailed.

"What a weird painting," I said. "And it doesn't really look right in here, does it?"

Patrick went quiet as he studied it closely.

"I agree, it does stand out," he said. "Usually every object that you find in an escape room has a purpose. Well, almost everything."

There was a clacking sound coming from the desk. Laurie had wandered off again.

"This typewriter is broken!" she shouted.

The three of us hurried over. The old typewriter had a sheet of blank paper rolled into it.

"Look," said Laurie. "If I press 'M' it says '7'!"

She hit the key with a whack and a 7 printed on the paper. I had a try. I had to hit the keys quite hard to get them to print, but every single one was wrong.

"The keys don't match up with what it's supposed to print," said Scout, looking confused.

I looked inside the top of the typewriter and gently held down the letter 'N'. The key lifted up and I could see that on the end was a metal stamp that said the number '3'.

"They've all been mixed up," I said.

"Someone could have done that deliberately!" said Patrick. He took the small piece of paper that Laurie had found in the shoe out of his pocket.

"Type in 'moon'!" he said. I did, but instead of printing the word, it printed some numbers.

"7553," said Scout. "What does some random numbers mean?"

Patrick was jumping up and down. "I knew it! I knew it!" he said. "This is *exactly* what an escape room is like. Clues like this! And those numbers aren't random at all. It's a code."

"A code?" I said. "A code for what?"

Patrick searched around the room but Scout was on to it immediately.

"The padlock on the trunk!" she said. She dived on

to the floor. "Yes! It needs four digits to open it. What were the numbers again?"

"7553," said Laurie, saying the numbers slowly in her special reading voice.

Scout put her face close to the padlock and scrolled the numbers into position. There was a very satisfying CLICK and the lock popped open. Scout unhooked the padlock from the catch and was just about to lift the lid when Patrick waved his arms.

"Stop!" shouted Patrick.

We stared at him, frozen. His face looked panicked.

"Edwina Patterson's rotting corpse might be in there!"

Scout dropped her hand. "What?" she said. "Of course it isn't!"

"But it might be! Well, not a corpse, exactly. Probably more like a skeleton. Wearing a dress or something."

"And no shoes!" said Laurie.

"Wouldn't there be a bad smell if that was the case?" I said quietly. All four of us sniffed the air.

"Oh, this is ridiculous," said Scout. "I'm just going to open it."

She took a deep breath, then very slowly, she lifted the lid.

CHAPTER TWENTY-THREE

"Waxing Gibbous."

I didn't think that Edwina Patterson's skeleton was going to be curled at the bottom of the old wooden trunk, but I still watched through squinted eyes as the lid opened. I wasn't close enough to see what was inside, but I could see the reaction on Scout's face. Her eyes widened and her mouth opened into a circle.

"Oh," she said. She reached inside and brought out a metal object which had a small brown label attached to it.

"What is it?" said Laurie.

Scout was turning it over in her hand. "I think it's a magnet," she said. She looked around for something to test the magnet on and then took the key to room forty-two out of her pocket. She put the key beside the magnet and it stuck, instantly.

"Yep, that's a magnet all right," said Patrick. "Can I have a look?"

He turned over the small brown label that was tied to the magnet with some white string.

"Waxing gibbous," he read.

"Waxing what?" I said. I held my hand out to take a look too. Patrick passed me the magnet. It felt heavy and cold in my hand. The words on the label were written in blue ink pen. It looked like the same handwriting as the 'moon' clue.

"Does anyone know what waxing gibbous means then?" I said. "Is it something to do with magnets?"

Scout shrugged.

Patrick was all fired up again. "Do you all agree that this room feels like a giant puzzle?" he said. "The 'moon' note, the adapted typewriter, the padlock and now a hidden magnet with a strange message. They were clues waiting to be found. Just like you suspected, Scout."

Scout smiled. Patrick took the magnet from me.

I was beginning to feel like there was something in this room after all. Two clues? That was too much to be a coincidence.

"I wonder if this maybe opens something else," he said. He waved it over the lock of the wardrobe, then tried the handle. It was still locked. Then he did the same over the little lock on the drawer of the desk, but that didn't open either.

"I don't think that is going to work, actually," said Scout. "I can't see it randomly opening a lock. Can you?"

Patrick turned to the three of us.

"OK. Let's look for something else that is related to the magnet then. Is there anything in the bedside cabinet?" he said.

Scout opened the top drawer and took out a hardback book. She turned it around to show us. My throat tightened when I saw what was on the cover. It was an image of a wolf, its nose pointing towards the sky as it howled. The title read:

Wolf Folklore

By Frederick Watkins

"It's a book about werewolves!" said Laurie.

"I don't get it," I said. "Does this have something to do with William Walters?"

"Maybe," said Scout. "He was here when she went missing. He must be a prime suspect."

Patrick frowned as he took the book from Scout. He flicked through the pages and shook it to see if there was anything hidden inside, but nothing fell out. Then he looked at the back of the book.

"It's all about wolves and the folklore behind them. Maybe this is a clue?" he said.

We looked at each other but no one could think of anything. Scout was chewing on her lip. "Maybe we should look at the book in more detail," said Scout.

"What? Read the whole thing?" said Patrick. "I'm not doing that!"

"But I've got to go in a minute and help Mum!" pleaded Scout. "You did say that most things in a puzzle room are used to solve the clues."

I took the book from Patrick.

"I can have a look through it later if you like," I said. "I'm quite good at noticing things so I might be able to help." Scout smiled at me. The walkie-talkie crackled.

"Right. We'd better go now," she said. "I've got

things I need to do for my mum." We all headed to the door.

"Don't you get fed up having to work in your school holiday?" said Patrick.

Scout frowned as she opened the room door. We all went out into the hallway.

"Of course I don't get fed up," she said. "This is my home, remember? It's not work. And I've only got three days to save it." She locked the door of room forty-two behind us and we made our way back to the red rope. Just then the lights flickered along the corridor and began to glow.

"Great. Mum must have sorted out the electrics," said Scout. "Right, I'll see you later at dinner if I'm not needed in the kitchen." She turned to me. "And take a good look through that book, OK, Todd?" I waved it at her and nodded.

When we got back to our room my heart leaped. Dad was sitting up in bed. He was leaning up against the headboard as he looked towards the window.

Laurie took a running jump and landed with a THWUMP on his bed, which gave a loud squeak.

"You're awake, Daddy!" she yelled with joy. "Todd and I have been on an adventure! We are solving a mystery and I found a shoe and Scout found a magnet and now we are trying to find a dead body!"

"Oh, have you now?" said Dad. "You *have* been busy." He stroked her fringe out of her face. Laurie was always talking rubbish so he probably believed that this was just another of her stories.

"And I found some more fossils!" she said. "Well, Scout found them for me."

"Cool," said Dad.

Fortunately she didn't mention that she'd run off to the beach. I wouldn't tell him either. I didn't want him to worry or feel bad.

Laurie scrambled off the bed and ran to our room. I heard her un-pop the lid of her tub of stones.

I glanced into the paper bag that Scout had filled with food. It looked like he'd eaten a sandwich and half of a piece of carrot cake. That was better than I had hoped.

"What is wrong, Dad?" I asked. "Why do you feel like this?"

Dad opened his mouth but nothing came out. I saw his eyes begin to fill with tears.

"I ... I ... can't explain it," he said, really quietly. "It's like inside ... something has been switched off."

It felt horrible seeing him like this and my stomach

twisted into a tangled knot.

"Is this the same thing that you had before?" I said. "When Aunt Lexie came over in the evenings after work?"

His chin trembled. Then he nodded.

"Are you sure you don't want to call a doctor?" I said. "Or Mum? I could tell her that it's not your fault and—"

"No. No, we don't need to worry your mum," he said, looking alarmed. "I just need to rest. That's what I did before, isn't it? I rested and then I was better. And look at me. I'm starting to feel better already."

He was right, he did look a bit brighter. And Mum definitely would worry. And what she was doing with her job was really important. I didn't think she could just up and leave it all and come home. And anyway, she was due to video-call us in a few days and if he wasn't better by then, I would tell her everything.

"Maybe we could all go down for dinner later?" I said. "I think the food here is really good." Dad's eyes looked panicked for a second.

"Um. I think I'll just keep resting for now," he said. He shifted in his bed and he slowly slid back down the headboard until he was flat again. My heart sank along with him.

"I'll go and see if Laurie is all right. We'll probably go and play on the beach in the rain or something," I said sarcastically.

Dad's eyes flickered towards mine.

"That sounds perfect, Todd," he said. "You both go and have a good time, won't you?"

He turned on to his side and closed his eyes. I glared at him. He had absolutely no idea about this hotel and what a mess it was. I imagined all of the hurtful words I could say. I could tell him about Laurie running off on her own to the beach. How bad would that make him feel? That he was too useless to even realize his own daughter had run off! But I didn't say anything. What would be the point?

In our room, Laurie was busy putting her fossils in a line on the lid of her tub. They might be pointless but they were good at keeping her quiet for ages.

I lay on my bed and looked at the cover of the *Wolf Folklore* book from room forty-two. It was very old, with a green cloth cover and embossed gold lettering. The first chapter appeared to be about stories of wolves in fables and religion. There were a few black-and-white drawings but nothing stood out as being a clue. I flicked through every page, running my eyes over the words to see if there was anything underlined or highlighted.

Then I spotted a chapter that was titled "The Mythology of the Werewolf". I turned the pages and stared at a black-and-white drawing of a wolf, standing on its back legs with its arms held up, claws pointing out. It would have been quite a scary picture, but the wolf was wearing a pair of trousers so it looked almost comical. The next page was all about the effect a full moon has on a werewolf, and then there was a diagram about the different phases of the moon. I spotted one that said 'First Quarter', which was the same as the writing on the clock in room forty-two. I was just about to turn the page when I spotted another moon phase. In this illustration, the moon was almost full, but there was still a shadow over a small area. Underneath the picture was a title. It said 'Waxing Gibbous'.

"That's it!" I said, sitting upright. "Waxing gibbous!"

Laurie jumped. "What is it?" she said.

"It's a phase of the moon," I said. "Scout was right. There was something in this book after all."

"Shall we find Scout now?" said Laurie.

"No. She's working, but we can tell her later," I said. Laurie yawned and went back to her stones.

I looked at the illustrations of the different phases of the moon in the book. It reminded me of a promise that Dad had made once, after he'd moved into his new house. For some reason, he got interested in astronomy.

"It's my new hobby!" he'd told us. *"And I'm going to go back to university and get a proper qualification!"* It seemed a bit odd as he'd never shown any interest in space before. Every time we visited there'd be more university brochures and prospectuses strewn across the kitchen table, and then one day, a huge cardboard box arrived containing a shiny, expensive-looking telescope. I was worried that Dad was spending money he didn't really have, but I had to admit, the telescope looked really, really cool.

"We can set it up in the garden and look at the moon!" Dad had said when I stared at the box in his lounge. *"Won't that be great, Todd?"* On the side of the box it read:

Bringing the universe into your own back garden!

There was a photograph of a boy and a man with the telescope all set up. The man, who I guessed was his dad, was smiling and pointing towards the stars. I asked Dad a few times about trying it out, but he seemed to lose interest in his new hobby as quickly as it had appeared. The cardboard box containing the telescope was pushed behind the large armchair and forgotten about.

I was just thinking about when we should go down for dinner when there was a knock on the door. Dad didn't stir and I only opened it a tiny amount, so whoever was there wouldn't see him lying in bed.

It was Scout. She was back in her hotel working clothes and she was holding a big tray of food.

"I'm not going to be able to chat, so I thought I'd bring your dinner to you," she said. "I thought your dad might be hungry so there's something for all of you." On the tray were cutlery, napkins, three glasses of juice and three covered bowls which smelled utterly delicious.

"Oh, wow. Thank you," I said, taking the tray. I was relieved that I wouldn't have to try and get a meal back for Dad. I was just about to tell her about the clue that I'd found in the book when she turned to leave.

"I've gotta go. Mum needs me!" she said, running down the corridor. "I'll see you tomorrow!" she shouted behind her.

Dinner was a vegetable stew and it tasted so good I wished I could have had a second portion. Even Dad had a few spoonfuls and he drank all of his juice.

After dinner Laurie and I both had showers and changed into our pyjamas. I was so tired I went to bed at the same time as Laurie and I didn't even notice the springs digging in my ribs. I must have fallen asleep pretty instantly.

The next day we went down for breakfast and I looked out for Scout so I could tell her about the clue I'd found in the book. There was no sign of her in the dining room. We saw Patrick on our way back through reception and he said he had seen her earlier, helping her mum, and that she'd see us later at dinner time. It sounded like they were really busy trying to keep the hotel going.

"Fancy going to the beach for a bit?" said Patrick shyly. "Dad's got some video calls this morning and I need to make myself scarce. It's stopped raining, at least."

Laurie gasped. "Can we, Todd?" she said. "Please?"

"OK," I said. "Can you wait here with Laurie?" I had some food for Dad so I quickly popped back to our room and put it on the bedside table. Dad was lying on his side and didn't stir. I suddenly wished he was coming with us to the beach. He was really good at skimming stones in the sea, making them glide across the water, jumping effortlessly from wave to wave. I wanted him to show me how to do it too. But there was no way he could do that now. I turned and headed back to reception.

Laurie, Patrick and I headed across the road to the beach.

We sat on the damp stones and Laurie immediately began to dig a hole with her hands.

"So, I had some data left on my phone and did another search on the internet for Edwina Patterson," said Patrick. "And way, way down on the searches there was a site that looked at old hotel stories. On it there was a discussion board where people were talking about their theories of what happened to Edwina Patterson, but they also mentioned rumours of there being some kind of lost treasure in the room. The last message had been posted years ago, but it does seem like there could be something hidden in there. I think we are definitely on to something."

"Brilliant!" I said. "I think I might have found something out too." I told Patrick about the reference to waxing gibbous in the *Wolf Folklore* book.

"That's it! That's the next clue, all right!" said Patrick.

We arranged to meet at six p.m. in the restaurant

to tell Scout what I'd found. Hopefully this time she wouldn't be too busy and we could get back into room forty-two.

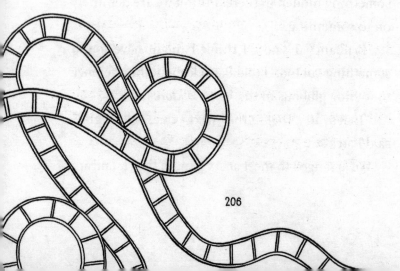

CHAPTER TWENTY-FOUR

"Oh, it's beautiful!"

It wasn't long until six p.m. came and it was dinner time again. Dad still didn't want to come with us and I promised I'd bring him back something nice to eat. I just hoped that Scout could help me.

I wasn't sure if any of the other guests would dress up for dinner. I thought that was the kind of thing people did in hotels, but I didn't know if that was just in movies. Laurie was still wearing the clothes she had been wearing since we had arrived, so I told her to change into something smarter. That's the sort of thing Mum would say.

I went to the bathroom and checked myself in the mirror. I looked OK. Tired, but OK. I wet my fingers and brushed them through my hair, then gave my face a wipe. When I came out into the bedroom, Laurie was wearing a pair of purple leggings and a yellow T-shirt. She looked like some kind of tropical flower.

"Ready!" she said. She had her tub of "fossils" under her arm.

When we got down to the dining room it felt like it had been completely transformed. Someone was playing a piano and the chandelier was glowing dimly. Every table was lit with a flickering candle, even though only three of them were occupied.

"Oh, it's beautiful!" said Laurie, looking around. And she was right. The twinkling light and the piano music gave the room a magical feel. I looked over at the black, shiny piano in the corner to try to see who was playing, but then Scout rushed over to us. She was dressed in a white shirt with black trousers and her heavy builder boots.

"Good evening, sir and madam! Could you step this way, please?" she said with a grin.

Laurie shuddered with excitement and her box of stones rattled.

"It's only us, silly!" said Laurie. "We aren't special!"

Scout pulled a puzzled expression.

"But of course you are special! You are our guests, so you will be treated with the utmost respect," she said. "This way! Please."

We followed Scout to a table near the kitchen door. Patrick and his dad were sitting at a table in the middle of the room, underneath the chandelier. Patrick waved at us and I waved back. His dad was looking at his phone.

There was another diner who was sitting in a dark corner on their own. Howard Knife. Standing next to his table and wringing a tea towel in her hands was Marianne Patterson. Howard was frowning and saying something and then he sipped from a glass of water. Marianne placed the back of her hand on her forehead, nodded at him, then rushed off to the kitchen.

"What's *he* doing here?" I said to Scout.

"The restaurant is open to the public so we can't stop him," she said. "And he's taking every opportunity to remind Mum that he'll have the contracts ready to sign tomorrow."

Howard spotted us looking and stared back.

"Just ignore him," said Scout. "The buffet selection is all over there." She pointed towards where we had got breakfast and lunch. This time the table was filled with pots of different hot food and bread rolls.

"By the way, I found something in the wolf book," I said. "Patrick thinks it's going to lead us to the next clue."

Scout's eyes glowed in the twinkling light and she grinned.

"I'll get you some water and then you can tell me all about it!" she said, before hurrying off to the kitchen door. Scout and her mum had clearly worked really hard to make this nice for everyone.

Laurie and I headed to the food. There wasn't a huge selection, but it all smelled incredible, just like our vegetable stew yesterday. I served myself some rice and vegetarian chilli and helped Laurie take a portion of fish pie and some salad. I carried our plates back to the table and sat back down. Scout reappeared with a jug of water and two glasses.

"Waitress! Waitress!" called a voice. It was Roland, Patrick's father. Scout rolled her eyes at us as she put our water and glasses down. She turned around.

"Yes?" she said rudely. She stomped over to their table with her hands on her hips.

"This pasta is undercooked," said Roland. He held up a fork of pasta covered with tomato sauce.

"How on earth can you serve undercooked pasta? It's so easy to cook!" He sat back in his chair and folded his arms. Patrick had his head down as he continued to eat.

"I'm terribly sorry, sir," said Scout. "Let me just check that for you, shall I?" She reached to his bowl, grabbed a tube of pasta in her fingers and popped it into her mouth.

Roland's eyes bulged and his face turned a furious red.

"Yep, it tastes just as I suspected," she said as she chewed, then licked the tomato sauce off her fingers. "The pasta is absolutely fine."

Roland looked very close to actually exploding.

"You . . . you just put your fingers into my dinner!" he yelled.

Scout just shrugged.

"Never in all my years have I ever seen such dreadful customer service," he bellowed. "You, young madam, are a disgrace!" Scout didn't flinch.

"And you, Mr Harris, are just an awkward customer who is rude to people to make you feel better about yourself. You are an angry man and no one will ever be good enough in your eyes. Isn't that right?"

Roland's mouth opened and closed a few times.

The room was silent as everybody watched. Even the pianist had stopped playing.

Roland gritted his teeth. "Tell your mother that we'll be checking out first thing tomorrow," he growled. He turned to his son. "Come on, Patrick. We're going."

Patrick put his fork down and I watched him blinking as he stared at the table.

"No, Dad," he said.

But Roland wasn't listening. "We'll get some decent food, then come back and pack," he said. "I'm afraid we'll have to endure one more night in this dump, but we can leave first thing." Roland stood up and put his blazer on, ignoring the fact that Patrick was still sitting there. Patrick shook his head.

"I'm not going," he said quietly. "I want to stay here."

Roland didn't appear to hear and took a couple of steps before turning around.

"Come *on*, Patrick," he said sharply. Patrick shook his head again.

"I like it here, Dad," he said. He looked up at him. "I like the people and the suite and the food ... and I like the music."

Roland looked confused for a moment and then

shook his head.

"Don't be ridiculous, this place is appalling. Come on and do what you're told." He made as if to leave, but Patrick still hadn't moved, so he just stood there.

"Scout was right," said Patrick. "You *are* angry all the time because . . . because it makes you feel better to put others down! It's not our fault that Mum met someone else. It's not my fault, it's not this hotel's fault and it's not *your* fault. You've just got to deal with it!"

There were a couple of awkward coughs from some of the other guests. Patrick picked up a bread roll that was sitting on a plate next to him and stuffed it into his mouth. His cheeks bulged as he stared at his dad.

Roland huffed then threw his napkin on to the table.

"We'll discuss this later," he said coldly. "I'll see you back in our suite."

He stormed across the restaurant and, after an awkward pause, the pianist began to play again.

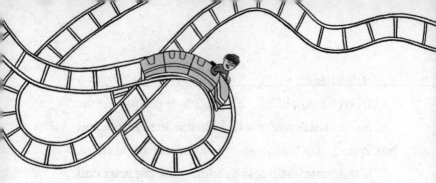

CHAPTER TWENTY-FIVE

"It's ... it's ... *him!*"

"Poor Patrick," said Laurie. We both looked over at him sitting at the table on his own. I did feel sorry for him. His dad seemed horrible. Laurie scrambled to her feet.

"PATRICK!" she yelled. "COME AND SIT WITH US!"

The other guests all looked round and a few of them tutted at their evening being disturbed by a family disagreement and now a yelling six-year-old. Patrick got up and slowly made his way over. He was still chewing the bread roll and had his napkin tucked into the front of his shirt.

"Hi," he said, sitting down opposite us. "Dad's a bit stressed tonight."

Laurie nodded and picked up a bread roll and bit on it.

"Is that true? About your mum making your dad angry all the time?" I asked. "Not that I'm being nosy or anything. It's just ... well, I know how it is when your parents split up."

"Yes," said Patrick. "Mum was seeing someone else behind his back and, well, I don't think he's got over it really. He wasn't like this before."

Laurie nodded as if she was a wise old lady rather than a six-year-old kid. "He must be feeling really very sad inside, don't you think?" she said.

Patrick seemed to think about it, but he didn't say anything. I don't think he wanted to talk about it any more. I knew what it felt like, too.

We ate our dinner, which was delicious. The hotel might be shabby and run-down but there was nothing wrong with the food. Scout and her mum were clearly brilliant chefs. The pianist came to the end of a song and there was a small smattering of applause from the other guests. Laurie, Patrick and I didn't clap as we didn't realize we were supposed to.

"Do you want ice cream?" said Scout, coming over

to us. "We've got butterscotch, pistachio or salted caramel. Mum made them."

"Yes, please!" said Laurie.

Scout looked at Patrick. "I'm sorry I yelled at your dad," she said. "We've been so busy and I'm just feeling worried about the hotel and everything. Are you all right?"

"Yeah," said Patrick quietly. "He deserved it. And you were right. The pasta was fine. He was just looking for another argument."

"Are you really going home tomorrow?" said Laurie. Patrick took a long breath.

"It looks like it," he said. "I guess I won't get to solve the mystery of room forty-two or find out what this magnet is for after all."

He took the magnet out of his pocket and placed it on the table.

"What was the clue you found, Todd?" said Scout, looking at me eagerly. "I *knew* there was going to be something in that book."

I had the book next to me and I opened it to the page with the illustrations of the phases of the moon.

"Apparently, the moon waxes and wanes. Waning means the moon that we see is reducing in size and waxing means the moon is getting bigger," I said.

"Waxing gibbous is a phase of the moon!"

"Yes, well done for spotting that, Todd!" said Scout. "Now we need to think what could be next. Any ideas?"

She looked at each of our faces in turn, as if waiting for one of us to suddenly jump up with the answer. But we were all deep in thought.

"I'll go and get the ice cream," she said. "Ice cream definitely helps with thinking." She headed back off to the kitchen.

Laurie suddenly let out a gasp.

"Look!" she whispered. "It's ... it's ... *him*." She lifted up her finger and pointed across the room. "It's the werewolf!"

Patrick slowly turned around and froze. William Walters was walking right towards us. His wide shoulders were stooped forward like he could quite easily drop to all fours and start running. Just like a wolf. I gulped.

He was almost at our table when Patrick turned back to us.

"Do ... do you think he's coming for me? Because I knocked on his door?" His face was drained of colour. He looked terrified. But I didn't get a chance to answer. William Walters had reached our table.

"You!" he said, pointing a long fingernail directly

at Patrick. "You said something earlier. About the music." His voice was deep and very gruff. A creepy old fairy tale where a wolf eats chalk to disguise his raspy voice suddenly popped into my head.

Patrick looked at me, confused. "Did I?" he asked. I shrugged.

"You did!" he barked. "You said you liked the music. I heard you."

Patrick looked utterly bemused. "Um. Yes, I guess so," he said. "I guess that was me."

William Walters nodded. I noticed he had hair sprouting out of the centre of his ears which was the same colour as his hair, eyebrows and beard. His mouth twisted into a strange kind of smile.

"Hmmm," he said. I looked down at the *Wolf Folklore* book on the table and I was just wondering if I could discreetly hide it when Laurie called out.

"Was that *you* playing the piano?" she said.

William took a step closer.

"It was," he answered.

Laurie pushed herself up on to her knees on her chair, just like she did when she was at home.

"It sounded pretty!" she said.

"Hmmmm," he said again. He looked like he was about to leave when he spotted the book on the table.

"Where did you get this?" he asked Patrick. He must have thought it belonged to him, as it was between the two of us. Patrick opened and closed his mouth, then looked at me, panicked.

"It's mine," I said.

William stared at me, not blinking. I had the feeling that he could tell I was lying.

He picked up the book and held it up close to his face. At first I thought his eyesight must have been bad, but then I saw a wrinkle on the bridge of his nose. He was ... *sniffing* it!

"Interesting," he said. He passed the book back to me and his thick eyebrows arched. He seemed amused. Then he reached for the magnet. Without saying anything he studied the label.

"Waxing ... gibbous," he read, very slowly. "A phase of the moon."

He knew exactly what it meant without having to find it in a book.

"That was the phase of the moon last night," he said. "And a beautiful one it was too." He looked at each of us in turn. "Did any of you see it?"

We all shook our heads silently. Then I saw Patrick's throat ripple as he swallowed. "You ... um ... seem to know an awful lot about the moon," he said. His voice got a bit higher as he spoke.

William's eyes narrowed to tiny slits. He slowly put the magnet back on to the table.

"I used to be a scientist, many years ago," he said, giving us the tiniest of smiles. "Did you know that there's going to be a full moon tonight?"

His nose twitched slightly, as if he'd caught the scent of something in the air, then he turned and stalked away.

Scout came out of the swinging kitchen door with a tray. She plonked four bowls of butterscotch ice cream down on the table and pushed a plastic tub towards me which had a fork balanced on top.

"For your dad," she said. "It's fish pie. It should stay warm for a bit. Is that OK?"

I felt a lump forming in my throat. It was strange how people doing nice things for you could make you feel like you wanted to cry. I hadn't even mentioned getting Dad food but Scout had already thought about it. I nodded and smiled at her. Scout sat down next to Patrick.

"We just met the werewolf!" said Laurie, a little too loudly. "He said there is going to be a full moon tonight! Do you think he's going to eat someone?"

"Laurie!" I said. "Don't be silly."

I took a mouthful of ice cream, which was soft and sweet and tasted of sugar and caramel. It was delicious.

"I already know about the full moon," said Scout. "I keep a note in my diary." I remembered now that I'd seen her on the night we arrived, standing on the steps of the hotel, staring at the moon.

"You don't really believe all this werewolf stuff, do you?" I said. I laughed but it came out more like a nervous chuckle.

Patrick sat forward.

"He *did* know what waxing gibbous means," he said. "Was there anything to do with the moon in room forty-two? We should be able to discover the next clue from that."

Laurie's spoon clattered in her bowl.

"The clock on the wall!" she squealed. "There was a picture of the moon inside it!"

"She's right. It didn't say waxing gibbous though," I said. "It said something like 'first quarter'."

Patrick's grin got even wider.

"That's good! We need to take a closer look at that clock," said Patrick.

Suddenly I got a tingling feeling in the back of my neck that someone was standing behind us. I turned around and Howard Knife was there, peering towards the magnet on the table. He walked around to take a closer look.

"What's that you've got there then?" he said. "And what is all this about a moon and a clock?"

"It's none of your business!" said Scout.

"You shouldn't be prying on other people's conversations!" said Laurie. "My teacher said that is rude, rude, RUDE."

Howard just sneered at her. I quickly picked up the magnet and slipped it into my pocket.

"You'd better not be taking that unlawfully," Howard said to me. "This hotel has been valued with the contents included. When I buy it, I will be checking every single nook and cranny to make sure there is nothing missing. You got that?"

I tilted away from him. He was so close I could smell his sour breath.

"No one is interested in you or your stupid attempt to buy this hotel, so why don't you just *bog off*!" said Scout. Laurie gasped and even Howard looked a bit stunned. He took a moment to compose himself, then put his hands on the table and leaned towards her.

"You don't realize that every time you insult me, you stupid, stupid child, I am going to knock thousands of pounds off my offer. You'll remember that when you've lost everything, won't you?" He stood back upright, then walked across the restaurant, disappearing out of the door.

"Do you think he heard us talking?" I said. "He might try and beat us to the next clue!"

Scout looked shaken. "No. He won't be able to get in there, not if we have the key. But I'm sure that whatever these clues lead to can help save the hotel."

"I agree," said Patrick. Then he told her about the internet search and the rumours of hidden treasure. This seemed to perk Scout up and she regained her confidence.

"The quicker we solve everything the better. Howard will be back tomorrow afternoon with the contract so we should go and look at the clock first thing tomorrow morning," she said.

Patrick sat forward. "But ... I'm going home tomorrow, remember?" he said. "Dad said we were leaving. And I can't see him changing his mind, can you?"

We went quiet.

"We'll have to meet later tonight, then," said Scout. "That means Patrick can help, and we need his brain. It also gives us a head start before Howard arrives tomorrow with the contract." She scraped the last of her ice cream on to her spoon and finished it in one mouthful.

"Later?" said Patrick. "How late?"

Her dark eyes shimmered in the light from the candle on our table.

"Let's meet at the red rope at eleven thirty p.m.," she said, getting up. "I'll see you there." She skipped across the room to collect some plates from another table, then headed to the kitchen.

Patrick, Laurie and I all looked at each other.

"I ... um," stuttered Patrick. "Do you think this is a good idea, Todd?"

I didn't like the sound of creeping around the hotel at night. Blake and Joe would call me Panic Button for thinking like that, but, all the same, it felt ... scary. But Scout was right; if we didn't go tonight then Patrick wouldn't be able to help. And he was the one who knew the most about these kinds of clues.

"It's *so* exciting!" said Laurie. "We're going on a night adventure!"

I glared at her. She was only six and yet she didn't seem to be worried about *anything*. I didn't think I'd ever felt like that. I chewed on my lip.

"So, are you going, then?" I said. "To meet Scout

at the red rope?"

Patrick got up and pushed his seat back under the table.

"Yep," he said. "I'm going to help her save the hotel. She needs me. See you there?"

I gave a non-committal nod and he made his way across the dining room towards reception.

Patrick hadn't mentioned the thing that was worrying me the most about creeping around an old hotel in the middle of the night. I didn't want to say anything in case I got laughed at, but surely Patrick had been thinking it as well? After all, William Walters had told us himself only a few moments ago.

Tonight, there was going to be a full moon. And *I* didn't want to be wolf food.

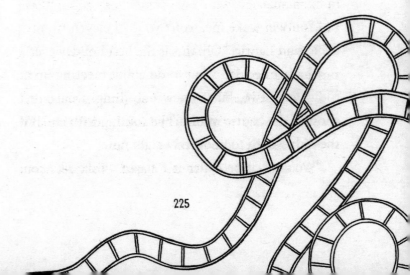

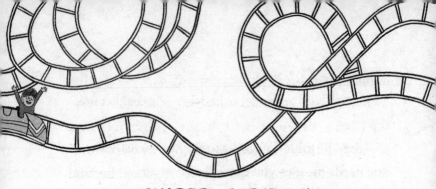

CHAPTER TWENTY-SIX

"You *will* wake me, won't you?"

Laurie and I made our way back to our room. I held the pot of dinner for Dad. It was still warm in my hands.

"You *will* wake me, won't you? At eleven twenty-five?" said Laurie. "Oh, this is the best holiday ever!"

I hadn't decided what to do about meeting up at room forty-two, but I knew one thing: whatever I chose to do, Laurie wouldn't be coming with me. But she didn't need to know that right now.

"Wouldn't it be better if I stayed awake like you,

Todd?" she said, scampering up the stairs. She caught her foot on a step and I grabbed her arm and steadied her.

"No, Laurie. You're tired already," I said. "If you get some sleep then you won't be all grouchy tomorrow."

"But I'm not tired!" she whined. I ignored her and turned down the corridor towards our room. I knew she'd be angry with me in the morning but I'd just have to deal with her tantrums then. We came to our door.

"Remember, don't say anything to Dad, OK?" I whispered. She nodded.

When we walked into the room my stomach did a loop the loop. The covers on Dad's bed were pulled back and there was a crumpled sheet where he had been sleeping. He was gone.

"Dad?" I called. "Dad!" I rushed into my and Laurie's room, but it was empty. Then I heard the sound of the shower running.

"Daddy's up!" said Laurie. "Yippee!"

My heart leaped. He must be better! He was probably cleaning himself up and having a shave!

I put his dinner on his bedside cabinet. Dad's phone was there and it lit up. Aunt Lexie was calling him. I picked it up and answered it.

"Hi, Aunt Lexie!" I said.

"Hi, Todd! Oh, it's so lovely to hear your voice. How

are you all doing? Are you all OK? Is your dad OK?"

I found myself feeling relieved that now I didn't have to lie. Everything was going to be all right.

"We're fine, Aunt Lexie. Everything is great! Dad's in the shower. How is your holiday?" I said.

There was a sigh from the other end of the phone.

"Oh, it's just *wonderful*, Todd. I've been to Rome! Can you believe it? Rome! It was so beautiful. We have been having the most amazing time."

I was grinning, even though she couldn't see me. But my face fell when the door to the bathroom opened.

Dad was standing wearing a T-shirt and boxer shorts. His eyes were sunken and hollow-looking and his cheeks looked gaunt and were covered in stubble. The fact that he'd got up and taken a shower didn't mean anything all. He was still ill.

"I really wish you were all here, Todd! It's just so incredible," said Aunt Lexie. "Hello? Are you still there?"

I cleared my throat a little.

"Yes, I'm still here," I said. "I wish we were there too." I felt a tightening in my throat but I tried to sound upbeat. "I'll, um, I'll tell Dad you rang, Aunt Lexie. Bye," I said.

I hung up.

I watched Dad as he slowly made his way back to his bed. He was moving so carefully it was as if every muscle in his body was aching. I didn't know what to say. He looked like he was in pain, but I knew the pain was coming from his head, not his body. He gave me a weak smile but he still hadn't said anything.

"I heard the shower and ... I thought maybe you were feeling a bit better?" I said.

"I just needed a wash," he said quietly.

I watched as he slowly crawled back into bed. His sheets looked rumpled and sweaty.

"I got you some food but the dining room is still open if you wanted to go downstairs to eat?" I said, trying to sound upbeat. "It's really nice down there. They've lit candles and there's a pianist."

Dad slowly shook his head.

"I'm not hungry," he said. He curled on his side and brought the duvet up so that it nearly covered his head. I stood there for a while, waiting to see if he would say anything else, but he was silent.

Laurie lay in bed, holding up a book but she wasn't reading.

"How long is it now? Until eleven twenty-five?" she

said, a little too loudly.

"Three hours," I said. "And keep your voice down." I was sitting on my bed and texting Mum about how much I was looking forward to talking to her in a couple of days. I was definitely going to tell her about Dad then, I'd decided.

"Should I get changed first or go in my pyjamas?" she said.

Considering there was no way she was going at all, it really didn't matter.

"I'd say your pyjamas will be fine," I said. "Now finish your book and get some sleep or you'll be too tired to go anywhere."

She shut the book with a snap and put it on her bedside table.

"Can you tell me a story, Todd? I don't think I can get to sleep. I'm too excited!" Her little feet kicked around under her covers.

"I don't know any stories," I said. I read my text to Mum and hit send.

"Tell me something about me when I was a baby!" said Laurie. "Something cute or something funny. Go on! *Please?*"

Laurie loved hearing about herself when she was really small, but there wasn't a great deal to say, apart from her crying a lot and being a pain.

"Um. . . Oh yeah, you used to have a cuddly giraffe that you carried *everywhere*. Mum bought it for you when we went to the zoo for your second birthday. You dropped it out of the buggy one day on the way home from school. You cried so much that Mum had to retrace her steps to find it. It had fallen in the road and been run over and it had a tyre mark across its middle, but Mum put it in the washing machine and you were happy again."

Laurie grinned.

"I remember giraffe! What was my birthday like at the zoo? Did I have a good time?"

I lay back on to my pillow and thought about it.

"I remember there was this really hot room filled with tropical plants and a little stream and there were all these butterflies flying around us," I said. "You had to look where you walked in case you accidentally trod on one."

"Did I like the butterflies or was I scared of them?" said Laurie.

"You liked them! You were in your buggy and you kept pointing as they flew around saying 'oooh'. All the other people there thought you were cute," I said. Laurie laughed at that.

"Oh! I remember something else now!" I said.

"While we were in there, this really big yellow butterfly landed on the top of your head and you had no idea! We didn't tell you in case it freaked you out. Mum took a photograph."

Laurie tucked her knees up and giggled.

"I want to see the photo!" she said. "That sounds funny." The picture was probably still on Mum's phone. This had been one of Dad's excitable 'rollercoaster' days. I remember him laughing so much about the yellow butterfly that a few people started staring at him.

"And what happened after that?" said Laurie. "What did we do next?" I stared at the blank wall opposite my bed.

"I can't remember," I said. Laurie waited.

"Did we see the other animals?" said Laurie.

"Yes. And then Mum bought you the giraffe and then we went home," I said abruptly. She frowned at me, puzzled at why I was suddenly snapping at her.

"What animals did we see?" she asked. "Were there lions? Or penguins?"

"I told you, Laurie, I can't remember," I said.

"But you said we saw the other animals so you must remember!" she whined.

"Laurie! That's enough! It's getting late. You'd

better get to sleep now or I won't be able to wake you up later," I said. I got up and turned her lamp off, then lay back down on my bed. I heard Laurie huff, then shuffle down under her covers.

"I liked hearing about the butterflies, Todd. Thank you," she said quietly.

While Laurie drifted off to sleep I tried to push the memory of the day at the zoo out of my mind. Remembering it was making me feel panicky inside, but it wouldn't go away. My brain just wanted to replay it all over again.

We had left the butterfly enclosure through some long plastic flaps and a mesh door that made sure none of them flew out too.

"Shall we go and look at the monkeys now?" said Mum.

"Yay!" said Laurie, kicking her little legs. Dad walked ahead, pushing her buggy.

We followed signs that pointed in the direction of the monkeys, but before we got there we came to a giant pirate ship surrounded by a low green fence. Above the entrance was a big red sign that said:

SHIP AHOY!

The ship looked amazing. It had three shiny silver slides of different lengths along the side I could see, and on the deck was a rope wall to climb and tunnels to crawl through. There were children everywhere, running up the steps and laughing and squealing as they bumped into each other to get to the slides first. Around the outside of the ship stood lots of anxious-looking parents.

Laurie spotted the ship and began pointing at it urgently.

"Ship!" she said in her toddler language. "Laurie go on? Pleeeease!"

Dad began to unbuckle the belt on her buggy, but Mum stepped forward.

"Dan, she can't go on there. Look. There's an age restriction," said Mum. There was a sign by the entrance.

Children must be supervised by a responsible adult at all times.
Not suitable for under 5s or over 12s.

She was right. Laurie was only two so she wasn't

allowed. But Dad had already picked Laurie up and she wriggled in his arms to get down and get to the ship.

"Ah, it'll be fine," said Dad. "She'll be with me! We're going to be *pirates*, aren't we, Laurie? Aaaaargh!"

Dad put on a loud pirate voice and a few parents turned to look at him.

"Dan?" said Mum. She frowned at him and I saw her do a tiny shake of her head. Dad blinked at her.

"Look, Dad," I said. "There's a toddlers' bit over there that Laurie can go on."

Through a gate in the fence was the entrance to an area called,

Little Captains!

I could see a smaller pirate ship with two plastic slides and a sandpit.

"Oh, that's better," said Dad, jiggling Laurie around. "We can go swashbuckling there, can't we?"

Laurie giggled and laughed and then Dad went galloping off towards the Little Captains area, like a horse.

Mum looked at me and gave me a weak smile.

"Come on, Todd," she said. "Let's go and watch, shall we?"

Seeing Dad fooling around with Laurie in the small playground was painful. He was so loud and kept putting on a silly pirate's voice.

"Shiver me timbers! I'll come and get ye with me cutlass, I will!" He pretended to chase Laurie, who was toddling around on the ground. She thought it was all hilarious, but that was just because she was too little to realize how embarrassing he was being. Mum and I stood on the outside of the playground. There was a couple beside us. The man had a baby in a carrier on his chest and the woman was holding a takeaway cup. "That poor kid, having a dad like that," said the woman as Dad lolloped around the playground, pretending he had a parrot on his shoulder.

"Who's a pretty boy then?" Dad said, to thin air.

The man beside us with the baby laughed.

"He's quite entertaining though, don't you think?" he said.

The woman shook her head. "More like quite embarrassing," she said. They walked away.

I reached up and held Mum's hand.

"Mum?" I whispered. "Can't you make him stop?"

Mum's face looked tense as she watched Dad.

As Laurie toddled towards the swings she tripped over and fell on to her tummy. She immediately began to wail and Dad quickly scooped her up. Fun time was over.

Dad cuddled Laurie and stroked the back of her head as he made his way to us. Mum rushed over to them and took Laurie in her arms, giving her a kiss on her cheek and wiping her eyes.

I looked around and noticed how everyone was staring at Dad, not just the couple with the baby. As he got closer to me I found myself wishing that he would just keep walking and that no one would know that this embarrassing man was actually my dad.

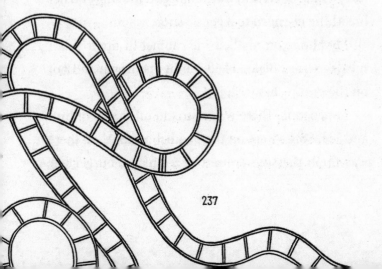

CHAPTER TWENTY-SEVEN

"It's just your imagination."

Laurie tossed and turned for a while, clearly excited about getting up late and going to investigate room forty-two, but eventually she stopped moving and her breathing changed to a gentle snore.

My phone on my bedside cabinet lit up. It was a message from Blake. He'd sent it just to me and not on the group chat with Joe.

I opened it. There was a stream of photos of him and Joe. Some were on the paddleboards, then there was them messing around at a cinema, burger bar and on the bus home. They looked like they were having a really good time.

Blake: How's the holiday going?
Any pics yet?

I thought about how I could answer. *Hi, Blake. Well, so far Dad hasn't got out of bed and I've been stuck looking after Laurie. She has run off twice so far, so that's going well. The hotel is a dump and practically falling down. The owner's daughter thinks there's treasure hidden in one of the hotel rooms and we're investigating a mysterious disappearance, potentially a murder. Oh, and there's a slight possibility that there is a werewolf staying here too. Bye!*

Instead I put:

Todd: It's great! Cool photos. See ya later.

I put my phone down and closed my eyes. I was so tired. I wondered what Patrick and Scout were doing; if they were planning on sleeping and setting an alarm or staying awake. But the more I thought about creeping around the dark corridors at night, the more scared I felt. I definitely wasn't going to go. What was the point? I was sure that Scout and Patrick would be able to work out what to do next. They didn't need me. But the next thing I knew I woke with a jolt. I was still lying on my bed, fully clothed. I must have nodded off. I looked over at Laurie, who had rolled off her pillow and had her arm dangling down towards the floor. Her mouth was open and she had a string of saliva hanging off her chin.

I picked up my phone. It was 11.27 p.m. I lay there, staring up at a strange brown stain on the ceiling. I looked around. The room seemed really light considering how late it was. I glanced over towards the door into Dad's room to see if he'd left a lamp on, but there was just darkness. Then I worked out why it was so light. The full moon.

I shuddered.

I thought of Blake and Joe's photos and all the fun they were having. And then I thought of Patrick and what he had said in the restaurant to his dad: that he didn't want to leave and that he liked it here. He must have had countless exotic holidays with his dad, but this grotty hotel was somewhere that he wanted to stay – and that was mainly because of the mystery in room forty-two. And Scout, I guess. She was kind of ... fascinating and like no one I'd ever met before. They would be expecting me to join them. But then there was a worry that was making my head thump a little: the story about William Walters being a werewolf and being locked in his room for one night each month. If that was true, then William would be bolted in his room right now, pawing desperately at the door as the full moon glowed teasingly through his window.

I shut my eyes and listened for anything that sounded like a werewolf. Maybe howling? Or pleading to be let out of his room? But all I could hear was the hushing sound of the sea rolling on to the shingle beach.

I guessed that Patrick and Scout must be there by now. I didn't move. I would just go back to sleep and wake up in the morning.

But then what? It would be another day worrying about Dad and telling more lies to Mum, Aunt Lexie, Blake and Joe. I could do that, *or* I could go and join Patrick and Scout and see if there really was a mystery to be solved in room forty-two. At least it would be something ... exciting?

I got out of bed and froze when a floorboard creaked. I held my breath as I tiptoed around Laurie's bed. Then I crept through Dad's room and out of the door. As soon as I got to the corridor I allowed myself to breathe normally. I looked down the dark corridor. I couldn't quite believe that I was going to venture out into this creepy hotel at this time of night. But what did I have to lose?

I very nearly went back to wake up Laurie. Not because I was scared, but because I wasn't entirely sure of the way to room forty-two and Laurie seemed to have memorized it perfectly. I knew I had to go up to the top floor, but after that the corridors twisted and turned like a labyrinth. The lights flickered as I walked, and I prayed that the electricity didn't go off. At one point I thought I felt warm breath on my cheek. I jolted around to check if there was a werewolf about to pounce on me, but the passageway was empty.

"It's just your imagination," I whispered to myself. "Just keep walking."

Eventually I spotted the bright red rope and felt a wave of relief. I'd found it! I stepped over the rope, then checked my watch: 11.34 p.m.

I gently tapped on the door. An unlocking sound came from inside and the door opened.

"You came!" said Scout.

She was back in her full werewolf protection gear: aviator goggles on top of her head, a long black coat and heavy boots. She locked the door behind me.

Patrick was by the clock, wearing a pair of navy pyjamas. They had his initials, PH, embroidered on the chest pocket.

"Hi, Todd," he said. "I think we need to somehow change the phase of the moon on the clock so it says 'Waxing Gibbous'."

"And how do we do that?" I said.

"Well, theoretically, if we can change the time then the moon phase should move on," he said.

I studied the clock on the wall and at the little painting of the moon with the swirling calligraphy that said "First Quarter".

Patrick pulled on the glass front of the clock case but it didn't budge.

"There aren't any hinges or catches," I said, looking more closely. "It doesn't look like it's meant to open."

"Maybe we need to get to the back?" Patrick said.

Scout put her hands either side of the clock and tried to lift it off the wall.

"It's fixed tight," she said as she tugged.

We stood and stared at the clock for a moment, thinking what to do.

"We could just smash the glass?" I suggested.

"No!" said Scout. "Can you imagine how much this clock must be worth? And if all this turns out to be for nothing I'd be in so much trouble."

Something Patrick had said about escape rooms popped into my head: when we had been looking at the strange painting of the fish that hung in the corner.

"Patrick? Didn't you say that most of the objects in an escape room have a use?" I said. My brain was whirring. "Where's the magnet?"

"I've got it," said Scout. She took it out of her coat pocket and passed it to me.

"What if the magnet can help us to open the case?" I said. "The label gave us the clue to where we need to change the setting of the moon. Maybe the magnet will show us how to do it."

"Well, go on," said Patrick excitedly. "Try it!"

I held the magnet to the side of the glass front of the clock. I could see there was a tiny hook on the inside, hooked over a little loop. When I placed the magnet close, it wiggled.

"I think it's working!" I said. "Look, the force of the magnet is making the hook move... If I can just get it to lift off then..."

I was close to lifting the catch when there was the sound of the hotel door being shaken violently. Someone was trying to get in.

"It's the werewolf!" said Patrick. "He's got out!"

CHAPTER TWENTY-EIGHT

"Let's see what's inside."

The three of us froze.

BANG, BANG, BANG!

Whoever was on the other side of the door was very, *very* angry. And they wanted to get in. . .

"It's him! I know it," said Patrick. "He's going to tear us all into pieces!" He looked like he might start crying and I didn't think I was far behind him.

Scout slipped her goggles down over her eyes.

"Who locks him in when there's a full moon?" asked Patrick, his eyes widening by the second. "You said your granny used to do it. Do you do it now?"

"Me?" said Scout. "No, of course I don't!"

"What about your mum?" said Patrick.

"I . . . I'm not sure," she said. "I think she does but I'm not supposed to know about him so I haven't asked."

"WHAT?" screeched Patrick. "I can't believe no one has locked him in! He's going to be in here any second. Quick! Look for something silver! That hurts werewolves, doesn't it? Silver? It burns their skin, I think! CAN ANYONE REMEMBER?"

The door began to tremble again, but this time it was caused by someone kicking at it.

"Patrick, calm down!" I said. "Scout just made the story up! It's not true! Is it, Scout?" I was feeling far from calm myself, but trying not to show it. I looked at her and she blinked at me behind the plastic lenses. She was about to say something when there was a voice behind the door.

"WHY DIDN'T YOU WAKE ME UP!"

There was another flurry of knocking sounds. Patrick's shoulders slumped with relief.

"I don't believe it," he said. "It's your sister!"

I went over to the door and let her in. She was red with rage and possibly only slightly less scary than an actual werewolf. She ran at me and shoved me in the stomach.

"You PROMISED!" she yelled. "You told me you'd wake me up and that I could join in but you didn't. YOU DIDN'T!"

She ran over to Scout and threw her arms around her waist and began to cry. Scout patted her on the head and glared at me.

"There, there," she said.

"Sorry, Laurie," I said. "I just thought you'd be too tired."

Laurie looked up at me through scowling eyes. I was going to pay for this, I could tell.

"Can we just get this over with?" said Patrick. "I want to get back to bed before an actual werewolf comes."

He still looked very shaky.

"Come on," I said. "Let's see if we can get the clock door open and change the time."

I went back to the clock and held the magnet where I'd put it before. The little hook trembled once more and I moved the magnet up, lifting the latch off the hook. I carefully opened the glass door.

"OK. Now we need to move the hands round and see if it makes the moon phases change in that little window behind the clock's hands," said Patrick. He was clearly itching to do it.

"Go on, Patrick," I said. "You try."

Patrick stepped forward and carefully put his finger on the big hand of the clock. He slowly began to move it round.

"I wonder how far I'll have to move the time forward?" he said. The time now said half past ten, then eleven, then half past eleven. The phase of the moon picture moved slightly around to the right.

"Keep going! It's moving!" said Scout. "I think once you get past midnight we'll almost be there."

Patrick kept winding the clock hands round and round and eventually, the first quarter phase of the moon was nearly out of sight in the little window. Edging its way into view was another picture of the moon with some different words underneath. My palms were sweaty as I watched. What was going to happen when it changed completely? The next phase-of-the-moon picture filled the small space and I read the words that were now revealed underneath.

"Waxing gibbous!" I said.

There was a click and then a tiny drawer at the side of the clock suddenly sprang open.

"Look! It worked!" said Scout. "It's a secret drawer!"

I reached into the drawer and took out another note, which was rolled up.

"What does it say?" said Laurie, forgetting her tears. I unrolled the piece of paper.

"It says LAMP," I said.

We all rushed over to the old lamp, which was on the cabinet next to the bed where Scout had found the book about wolves. The lamp had a round, golden base and a bright yellow shade with tassels along the edge. I looked around for any clue.

"There's nothing here," I said.

"Try underneath it?" said Scout. I lifted the lamp up. It was heavy and had left some scratch marks on the wood, but there was nothing else of note.

Patrick sat down on the bed.

"It must mean something," he said. "Maybe the clue has been lost."

Laurie went over to the lamp. She reached down the side of the cabinet to a wire and with a click she turned the lamp on. The lamp glowed yellow, revealing the silhouette of a small key that had been taped on the inside of the shade.

"A key!" I said. "That's so clever! Well done, Laurie." My sister grinned at me, then quickly narrowed her eyes again, remembering I was still the worst brother in the world.

Patrick turned the lamp off, then reached under

the shade for the key and pulled it away. It was small and looked like it was made of brass.

"Right, now we need to find something else to unlock," said Patrick.

"I know!" said Laurie. She ran to the wardrobe and pointed to the hole, which looked to be the perfect size.

We hurried over to the large wooden wardrobe and Patrick put the key in the lock. We held our breath. It fitted perfectly. He was just about to turn it when Laurie let out a little squeal. He stopped.

"What if the werewolf got Edwina and he spat the bones out and hid them in there?" she said.

I sighed.

"Just open it, Patrick," I said.

He turned the key and slowly opened the doors. There were a few empty clothes hangers on a single rail, but I couldn't see anything else.

"There's a box!" said Laurie. She crouched down and her arms stretched into a dark corner. She brought out a small brown box which fitted between her two small hands. Laurie looked up at us.

"Well go on, Laurie," said Scout. "You found it, so you can open it. Let's see what's inside."

Laurie took a deep breath, then carefully lifted off the lid.

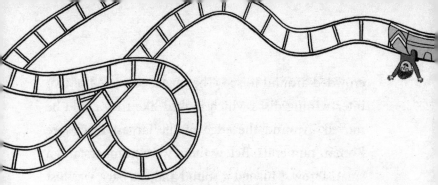

CHAPTER TWENTY-NINE

"But what is it?"

Laurie's face began to glow, not from the excitement of being up late and solving clues in a creepy hotel room, but because whatever was in that box was giving off some kind of light. I pictured a pile of diamonds and gemstones twinkling back at her. Had we found the treasure? Already?

Laurie's jaw dangled down as she reached inside the box.

"It's so beautiful," she said. But it wasn't diamonds or jewels. It was a golden, circular, flat object about the size of my palm. She held it up and we crowded around to see. The object consisted of two intertwining discs which looked like they could be moved. Around the edge of the largest disc were Roman numerals. Below them were numbers and a small arrow. I turned it round and the back was just as ornate. Laurie began to fiddle with the dials.

"Stop!" shouted Patrick. "Don't move anything. It could be important how it's been set."

Laurie quickly moved the dials back to their original position. Fortunately, she hadn't moved them too much.

"But what is it?" she said. Patrick took it from her for a closer look.

"I've no idea," he said.

"Is it some kind of compass? Or another type of clock?" asked Scout.

"Can I see?" I asked. Patrick passed it to me. The dials were flat and intricately designed. "It looks like it's something scientific to me," I said. "Was there anything else in the box, Laurie?"

She checked, then took out a small piece of wood and gave it to me. There was a groove cut into the wood and the circular-dialled object fitted perfectly inside.

"It's got a stand so it must be an object that is put

on display," I said. I walked over and placed it on the desk. It looked very clock-like but it definitely wasn't for telling the time.

Laurie gave a really big yawn. When she saw me looking she quickly closed her mouth, pretending that she actually wasn't tired in the slightest.

"I think we should all get back to bed," I said. "Maybe we can come up with some ideas tomorrow."

"But I'm going home, remember?" said Patrick.

"And Howard Knife is coming back with his stupid contract," said Scout, wiping her forehead.

I picked up the gold object and put it back into the cardboard box, then gave it to Scout.

"I know who might be able to help," I said. "William Walters."

"What?" said Patrick. "Maybe it is a good idea I'm going home after all. There's no *way* I'm going near that old man. He's dangerous!"

"But he's a scientist!" I said. "He told us. He knew all about the phases of the moon. I bet he knows about these kinds of scientific instruments and what they're for."

"Hmmm," said Patrick. "Or *maybe* he's the kind of scientist that likes cutting up bodies … with his own hands!"

"Patrick is being slightly hysterical, but he's right,"

said Scout firmly. "I think it's probably best you don't disturb him or make him angry."

Patrick shrugged. "Yep. Better to be alive and hysterical than wolf dinner." He made his way to the door. "Are you coming? I don't fancy walking these corridors on my own again."

We all followed him out of room forty-two and Scout locked the door behind us. She still had the cardboard box under her arm.

"Let's meet in the morning at breakfast," she said quietly. "We can decide what to do then. And then we can say goodbye to you, Patrick. Unless you can change your dad's mind?"

We began to walk slowly down the corridor. Patrick grunted.

"Fat chance of that happening," he said. "I don't think anyone has changed Dad's mind, *ever*."

We walked along for a little while and then Scout left us, turning in another direction.

Laurie suddenly trotted to walk beside Patrick. She reached for his hand again.

"Patrick?" she said. "Why don't you tell your daddy that you want to stay?"

Patrick thought about it for a moment and then he sighed.

"He won't listen," he said sadly. "He's always too busy with work."

"My teacher said that we listen best when we don't have any other distractions," she said. "Maybe tell your daddy when he just *has* to listen?" She swung his hand back and forth as they walked.

"Your teacher sounds very wise," said Patrick, "but she's not met my dad."

We got to his suite and he nodded at us and waited for us to pass, before he silently slipped back into his room. It would be a shame if Patrick had to go home. He was clearly very good at solving puzzles and, the more time he spent with us, the nicer he became. I got the feeling that he was stressed when we first met him, purely because of his dad.

As we carried on our way back to our room, I noticed Laurie stumble a couple of times. I picked her up and she instantly rested her head on my shoulder. I placed my hand on the back of her head as I walked and I felt her warm breath on my neck. She was a complete and utter pain, but she was still my little sister.

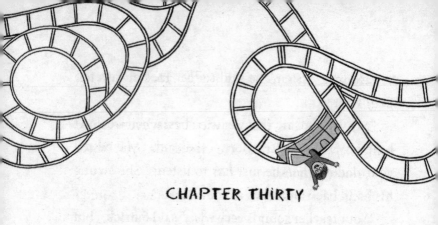

CHAPTER THIRTY

"*I'll* talk to the werewolf."

The next morning, I woke up late. Laurie was still snoring and I quickly got showered and changed. I didn't want to miss meeting up with Scout and Patrick at breakfast and hoped they would wait for me. But when I was brushing my teeth, there was a knock on our door. Laurie was stirring and she blinked at me with dazed eyes.

"Get dressed, Laurie," I said. "There's someone here."

I rushed into Dad's room. He was in bed, staring at the ceiling.

"Dad," I said, going over to him. "There's someone

at the door. Did you hear them knocking? What shall I do?"

Dad looked at me. It was as if every word completely puzzled him. He closed his eyes. There was another knock.

"Hello? Mr. Franklin? It's Marianne here. Could I have a quick word?"

It was Scout's mum. What did *she* want? I went over to the door.

"Um. Hello? Can I help you?" I said.

"Is that Todd? It's Marianne here. Can you open the door, please?" she said.

I hesitated but knew I had to do something. I quickly ran to Dad's bathroom and turned on the taps of the bath. They made an overhead shower start working and the water shot out, splashing on my arm.

I went back to the door and opened it just a crack so that she couldn't see inside. Her smile dropped as I peered at her through the gap. She tried to see over my head.

"Hello. Is everything all right?" she said, still trying to see past me. "It's just that I noticed the do-not-disturb sign is still on your door and we usually do a daily freshening up of guest rooms."

I glanced down at the cardboard sign.

"We don't need anything, thank you," I said.

"There isn't any damage to the room, is there?" she said. "You're not hiding anything? Is your dad there? Can I have a word with him, please?"

"No, nothing's damaged," I said. "And Dad's in the shower at the moment." The sound of the shower splashing in the bathroom was pretty clear. Surely she wouldn't suspect I was lying? Marianne's face looked strained and she didn't seem happy or as warm as she had been when we arrived. I guessed it was the stress she was under with Howard Knife on her case.

"I can get him to pop down and see you later if you like?" I instantly regretted it. Why had I said that? There was no way Dad was going anywhere.

A small body pushed round me and through the gap in the door.

"Hullo!" said Laurie. She'd changed out of her pyjamas and into a pair of red shorts with a navy-blue T-shirt that had the word "Twinkle" written on the front in sparkling silver letters. Under her arm was her plastic tub. "We are having a brilliant holiday!" she said to Marianne.

"I'm so happy to hear that!" said Marianne, brightening a little.

"Do you want to see my fossils?" said Laurie.

"Maybe another time," said Marianne. "We'll be clearing away the breakfast things soon so you might want to get down to the dining room quick."

The thought of missing breakfast made Laurie forget all about her fossils. She rushed back inside to get her shoes on.

"Right, well, I'd better be going. I wouldn't want to miss breakfast either," I said. I was about to close the door when Marianne put her hand against it.

"Are you sure everything is OK?" she said. "We haven't seen your dad since you've been here and I wouldn't want to think you are on your own or anything."

"What?" I said, laughing. "No. We're not on our own. Dad is just catching up with some sleep. He's been working really hard and, like I said, he's in the shower right now or he'd come and say hi."

Marianne nodded and her warm smile returned.

"OK," she said. "Well, you know where we are if you need us."

I grinned back at her and laughed as if to suggest that *us* needing *help* was utterly hilarious.

"No problem. Bye!"

I quickly closed the door and rushed to our room to put on my trainers. I didn't want to miss breakfast or meeting Scout and Patrick. Unless Patrick had left already of course. I really hoped he was still around and he'd even managed to persuade his dad to stay.

I went to Dad's bed.

"We're going for breakfast now, Dad," I said. "Do you want to come?"

Dad slowly shook his head.

"No, Todd. Not now," he said.

"Fine, so what do you want to eat then?" I snapped. "Toast? Or there's cereal? Did you want coffee or tea? Orange juice?"

Dad flinched against the questions as if each one was a pebble being flung at him, stinging his face.

"I ... I don't care," he said. "Just get anything."

He rolled away.

"Come on, Laurie," I said loudly. "Looks like we're on our own *again*."

When we got to the dining room, Scout and Patrick were the only people there. They both stood up when Laurie and I walked in.

"Hey, sleepyheads," said Scout.

"Hi!" said Patrick brightly. "Guess what? I'm staying!"

Laurie squealed and clapped her hands.

"That's brilliant!" I said. "Did your dad change his

mind then?"

Patrick nodded.

"Yep," he said. "I did what you suggested, Laurie."

Laurie looked surprised. "Me?" she said.

"Yes! You said that people listen better when they don't have distractions, so I hid Dad's phone before he woke up!" he said.

"Blimey," I said. I could picture Roland Harris's angry face when he realized what Patrick had done.

"Did he go mad?" Scout asked.

"I didn't give him a chance!" said Patrick. "I sat on his bed and told him that I was having a really good holiday and I'd made some friends and that I wanted to stay. And ... after a bit of huffing and puffing ... he said yes! He didn't shout or anything. He said he won't use his phone today and he's going to take a day off work. He even suggested we go for a walk on the beach this morning."

Laurie smiled. "That's brilliant, Patrick," she said.

"And what about the clue?" I said. "Has anyone got any ideas what that object is that we found?"

"Nope," said Patrick. "But I think that you're right, Todd. We need to ask William Walters if he knows what it is. We are running out of time and I'm stumped!"

"Great. When can we see him?" I looked at Scout

and back at Patrick. They exchanged a glance.

"That's the problem," said Scout. "Patrick is going out with his dad and I've got to clean two rooms and keep Mum away from Howard Knife. He's coming back today and I've got to be around to make sure that Mum doesn't sign anything."

"Dad never asks me to do stuff with him so I can't say no," said Patrick. "Just pop to room thirteen and ask William if he knows what this thing is. OK? Easy."

Patrick had the box containing the gold object in his hands. He shoved it towards me, forcing me to take it.

"Me?" I said. "No way! I'm not doing that." I tried to pass the box back to Patrick but he folded his arms and grinned. He seemed to be finding the whole thing quite amusing.

Scout raised her eyebrows.

"Todd, you've said yourself countless times that he's not a werewolf. It's not like you're frightened or anything, is it?" She had a smirk on her face.

"Of course not!" I said. "I just think it's a bit rude to knock on his door and ask for help. And anyway, Patrick should do it. He likes Patrick because he said he liked his piano playing."

"I'll do it," said Laurie. We ignored her.

"He doesn't *like* me, he wants to *eat* me!" said Patrick. "There is a difference, you know?"

Laurie grabbed me on the sleeve.

"*I'll* talk to the werewolf," she said.

I shrugged her off and then looked around the empty dining room. "Isn't he here having breakfast? Can't we ask him now? All of us?"

"No. He never eats breakfast," said Scout.

"That's surprising after he's been locked in his room all night," said Patrick, clearly finding this all highly amusing. "I bet he'll be extra hungry when he sees you, Todd."

Laurie tugged on my arm again and I pulled it away. She huffed, then stomped off towards the breakfast buffet.

"I don't think it's a good idea," I said. "I mean, what if he gets angry with me for bothering him?"

Scout looked irritated. "But Todd, solving these clues might be the only chance we have to save the hotel. To save my home," she said. "I thought you were going to help?"

I could feel the panic rising in me. It was like I was climbing up the steep hill on that rollercoaster again, getting ready to plummet. How would I know which way it was going to go if I couldn't see far enough ahead?

I looked at Scout and she glared back at me.

"Oh, just forget it," she said. She turned and marched off to the kitchen. I felt a mix of embarrassment and relief at the same time. There was an awkward silence at the table and then Patrick jumped up as he spotted his dad.

"Hi, Dad!" called Patrick across the dining room. His dad was carrying their matching anoraks. He smiled at his son, but then his phone rang and he fumbled to answer it and hurried out of the room, his voice booming loudly: "ROLAND HARRIS SPEAKING."

Patrick looked at me and shrugged.

"I guess it must be a really important call," he said. He walked over to his dad, his head hanging a little lower.

I went to the breakfast buffet to get something to eat but there was no sign of Laurie. I assumed she had still been deciding what to eat. Where had she gone now? I put the contraption from room forty-two into my hoodie pocket.

I quickly drank a glass of orange juice and picked up a banana and a cereal bar for Dad. I buttered some toast and ate it as I walked back out into reception.

Howard Knife was sitting on the scruffy sofa, looking over some paperwork. He was here already? Did Scout know? His eyes looked over the top of the paper and narrowed when he saw me. I frowned back at him, then ran up the stairs. As I hurried along the corridor, I checked behind me a few times that he wasn't following.

Back in our room I dropped the cereal bar and banana on to Dad's bed.

"There's no coffee," I said. Dad turned and smiled at me, but I didn't smile back. Maybe if he wasn't being waited on he'd be more interested in actually getting up? I went into our room, expecting to see Laurie sitting on her bed, moody with me for ignoring her. But she wasn't there. I sat down with a huff. I seemed to be spending most of my time running around for my family and I was fed up with it. I looked at Laurie's glass of water on her bedside table and the space where her tub of fossils usually sat.

I remembered that Laurie had been tugging on my sleeve when we'd been talking about William Walters. I groaned when I realized exactly where she had gone. She'd gone to room thirteen to visit the werewolf, all on her own.

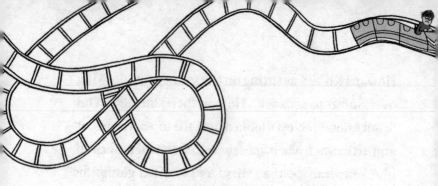

CHAPTER THIRTY-ONE

"I think you're just different."

My stomach churned as I walked towards room thirteen. What was she thinking, going off like that? I kept an eye on the room numbers as I walked, then turned a corner and into the corridor where room thirteen was. I could see Laurie, standing at the door, talking to someone. I hung back a bit. It sounded like she had only just got there.

"You know that you said that you are a scientist?" she said in her high-pitched, excited voice. "I thought you might want to look at my fossils."

I cringed. What was she *doing*?

"Hmmm," growled William. He didn't sound too happy about being disturbed, but that didn't put off my little sister. She began to pull off the lid of the tub.

"You can look at them but you've got to be very careful as they are extremely valuable and *precious*," she said.

I stepped forward.

"Laurie!" I hissed. "What are you *doing*?"

Laurie jumped when she saw me, then she regained her composure.

"This is my brother, Todd. He's scared of you, but I'm not," she told William Walters.

"Laurie!" I said again. I glanced up at the big man, who was scowling under his heavy, thick eyebrows. He was wearing the same suit he had on when Patrick knocked on his door. As I glanced down at the cuff of his sleeve I saw something dark and red on the fabric of his shirt. It looked like blood. I felt like I wanted to throw up my breakfast.

"I'm sorry my sister disturbed you," I said. I grabbed Laurie by the arm. "Come on, we've got to get going."

"Hang on," said William. "Let me take a look at those fossils before you go."

Laurie wrenched her arm free, giving me her angry stare, then looked up at William, her face beaming.

"Let me see now," said William, peering into the tub. He reached his hand in and pushed the stones around with his long yellow fingernails.

"What do you think?" said Laurie. "They're very special, aren't they?"

I waited for William to bring her world crashing down. To tell her what I'd been saying for months – that the tub was filled with stupid pebbles and she was deluded. But instead his face stretched into a kind of smile.

"Very interesting," he said. He picked up a stone, studied it closely, then put it back and picked up another. "Very interesting indeed."

He stopped and looked at Laurie. "And you'd like to be an archaeologist one day?" he said.

Laurie shrugged. "Maybe. Or I want to own an ice cream van and drive around the whole world, selling ice creams."

William made a strange noise, like a deep chuckle. He was laughing!

"I see," he said. "They both sound like good options."

He stopped looking at the stones and looked at the two of us. I looked away – still embarrassed that my sister had told him I was scared.

"Come on, Laurie," I said. "Let's go now."

Laurie put the lid back on to the tub of rocks.

"My brother has got something to show you too!" she said brightly. "We found it. It's extremely crucial as we are solving a puzzle. Show him, Todd!"

I quickly looked at William. He was frowning again.

"What's that then?" he said. "Come on now. I'm a busy man."

He didn't seem as friendly to me as he did with Laurie and I quickly took the strange object out of my hoodie pocket.

"Um. It's this," I said. "We are ... um ... working on a school project."

William took the object and held the discs up to his face, peering closely at the inscribed numbers. The gold colour reflected in his eyes made them glow a light shade of amber.

"Now this is rather marvellous," he said. He looked at both sides and then carefully moved one of the dials. I remembered what Patrick had said about the numbers being important.

"Um, can you not move those, please?" I said. William froze and looked up at me, his forehead knitted together in a deep frown.

"It's just that . . . um. We think the numbers might be relevant to something, you see," I muttered. "We need to find out . . . for a school project."

William nodded at me, then turned the dial back to its original position.

"I know what this is," he said. "But I've only ever seen one in a museum."

He handed it back to me. I tried to hold his gaze as he stared right at me. I knew he was trying to intimidate me because he thought I was scared, and he was doing well.

"What is it?" said Laurie. His eyes broke away from mine.

"It's a tidal abacus," he said.

"A tidal abacus?" I said. "What's that?"

William turned it around to face us.

"These discs make up a lunar calendar. You use the dates to work out the position of the moon and on the other side is the tidal clock, which will tell you when high and low tides will be."

Another clue linked to the moon! Patrick and Scout would be really interested to hear that.

"High and low tides are controlled by the moon's gravitational pull," he continued. "This is a tool to calculate those tide times by adjusting the discs to the phases of the moon."

"Ah. So, it's kind of like a calendar?" I said.

William gave me a quick nod. I could tell he'd had enough of our questions now and was getting ready to shut the door.

"Can I ask you something?" said Laurie loudly. She took a step closer to him. I knew exactly what she was going to ask and I quickly tried to head her off before she said any more.

"We'd better go now. Come on, Laurie," I said, light-heartedly. "Thank you for your help, Mr Walters."

But Laurie didn't budge. She was almost over the threshold of the door, inside his room.

"Is it true that you are an actual real-life werewolf?" she said in a hushed voice.

William Walters froze as he stared at her. His nose twitched slightly and then his sharp eyes darted to look directly at me.

"And what do you think? It's Todd, isn't it?" he said. "Do you think I'm a werewolf, Todd?"

I stared back at him and managed to hold his gaze without looking away. I thought about Dad then and how Dad's moods made him sometimes seem like a different person. I thought about how those people at the zoo playground had looked at him like he was some kind of creature from another planet. But they didn't know him.

"Um," I said. "I think... I think you're just different. And maybe people have just assumed things about you that aren't true."

I took a deep breath. He nodded at me.

"Good," he said. He looked back at Laurie.

"This tidal abacus is a very interesting scientific instrument," he said. "And you got this from your school, you say?"

I was about to say yes when Laurie jumped up and down.

"It was in room forty-two!" she said. "We think there's a dead body in there!"

William raised his eyebrows at me.

"That's not quite right," I said. And then I told him about the disappearance of Edwina Patterson and how the room appeared to be full of clues waiting to be solved. I explained that Scout wanted to try and find out what was hidden in there because she was trying to save the hotel.

"Ah, I assumed Scout was behind all of this," he said. "She has a great imagination, that one. I see her running around the hotel with all these strange ideas in her head. She'll make a good novelist herself one day. Just like her great-great-grandmother."

I agreed with him. Scout was certainly good at telling a story.

"Thank you for showing me your fossils, Laurie. And thank you for not believing I'm a werewolf, Todd," he said. He chuckled to himself, but at the end he made a low howling noise. He twitched his nose again, then closed the door.

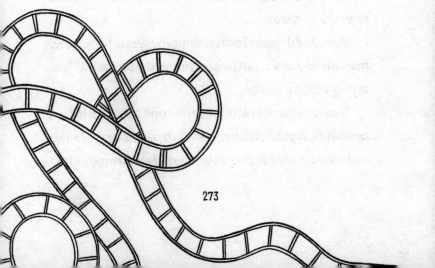

CHAPTER THIRTY-TWO

"It's just a silly fish."

"That was the absolute last time you run off, Laurie," I said as we walked down the corridor. "Do you hear me? I'm going to text Aunt Lexie and Mum and tell Dad and we are going to leave this hotel if you ever, *ever*, do it again."

"Yes, Todd," said Laurie, skipping along beside me, her tub of fossils rattling. I stopped and pulled her arm so she faced me.

"I'm serious. If you do that just one more time, this holiday is absolutely over, do you understand?" I said.

Laurie pulled up her shoulders and scowled at me.

"Todd!" It was Scout. She was in her full "investigating" outfit, including goggles on the top of her head. "How is it going? I'm free for a while."

"We met the werewolf!" said Laurie. "I showed him my fossils and Todd showed him the thingy. He said it's to do with the sea!"

Scout looked interested.

"The sea?" she said. "How?"

"It's a tidal abacus," I told her. "It uses the phases of the moon to work out when there are going to be high and low tides. Is there anything in the room to link it to? I've been thinking about it but I can't remember anything in there to do with the ocean."

Laurie gasped.

"The fish painting!" she said.

"Yes!" I said. "Brilliant. Can we go and take a look?"

"Absolutely!" Scout said.

"Oh, and did you know that Howard Knife is already here? I saw him in reception," I said.

"Yes," said Scout. "I saw him too. I need to make sure Mum doesn't sign anything so I hid all the milk and she's gone off to the shops to get some more for the guests. She won't be long though so we've got to hurry. I'll contact Patrick." She took her walkie-talkie out of her pocket. "His beach walk didn't go

275

to plan so I gave him Mum's receiver and said we'd let him know when we're ready to go to the room."

Poor Patrick. His dad's promise to spend time with him didn't seem to have lasted very long.

She pressed the side button.

"Scout to Patrick. Scout to Patrick. Over."

We all waited. There was a crackle and then the sound of someone laughing.

"This thing is ancient! Haven't you heard of mobile phones?" There was a pause, then Patrick said. "Oh, and over!"

"We'll meet you at room forty-two," said Scout. "The object was a tidal abacus. We need to take a look at that fish painting. Over."

"OK. I'm on my way. Over!" said Patrick.

We all arrived at the room at the same time.

"You OK, Patrick?" I said. Patrick shrugged.

"Yeah, I guess," he said. "We walked for a little bit but then Dad had to sort some urgent work out. I can't stop him working, can I?" He looked sad for a moment, then he stood up a little straighter.

"Anyway, this is much more important than walking on the beach in the pouring rain. Come on. Let's go in and see if there are any more clues in that weird painting of a fish," he said.

276

But when we stepped into room forty-two, it was dark. Very dark.

"Someone has closed the curtains," said Patrick. "Scout? Did you do that?"

Scout shook her head.

"Maybe Mum has been in here," she said. She walked over and slowly opened one of the curtains. Light flooded the room. It had stopped raining and dust particles floated in the strip of yellow sunlight.

"Right. Let's take a closer look at the painting," said Scout. "And then I think we'd better get out. Mum will be back from the shops soon and she might sign that contract if I don't stop her."

We went to the picture and looked at it closely.

"What are the numbers on the tidal abacus, Todd?" said Patrick. I held it up and looked closely at the intertwining discs and where the dials were pointing.

"One arrow is pointing to the number 1," I said. I turned the abacus around. "And on this side the dials are pointing to roman numerals. It says XXVIII."

"Twenty-eight," said Patrick without any hesitation or attempt to show off.

"Is there anything on the painting with those numbers?" I said.

We all stared at it. The eye of the fish bulged back

as if it was staring at us too.

"It's just a silly fish," said Laurie.

"Can we take it off the wall and see if there's anything on the back?" I said to Scout.

"Sure," she said.

Patrick reached for the painting and was about to lift it off the wall when there was a loud creak from behind us. We all spun round. Standing in the dark shadows by the wardrobe was a figure.

"Who's there?" shouted Scout.

"It's the werewolf!" quivered Patrick, and he pressed himself up against the wall. But it wasn't William Walters. Stepping out into the daylight was Howard Knife. "It's the bad man!" shouted Laurie.

"What are you doing here?" said Scout.

Howard walked towards us, a smile on his face.

"I'm just having a look around at what will soon be mine," he said. "Your mum *is* going to sign the contract. You *do* know that, don't you? And whatever is in this hotel, and this *room*, will soon be mine too. So go on, tell me. Where is Edwina Patterson's treasure? Someone has left clues, haven't they?"

Scout folded her arms.

"I have no idea what you are talking about," she said.

Howard laughed. "I saw you all hiding under

the bed that day. Remember? I knew you were up to something. It only took a quick search on the internet to find out that there's *something* in here."

"Yes!" said Laurie. "And the clues are WAY too difficult for you to solve!"

My heart sank. She'd given Howard all the confirmation that he needed.

"Aha! So there *are* clues," said Howard. Laurie bit on her bottom lip. "Anyway. It's no odds to me. I can just rip everything out and find it once this place is mine."

"Mum won't ever sign. You're wasting your time," Scout said.

Howard snorted. "Remember, I've seen what a state your accounts are in. I think your mother confuses running a business with running a charity. Letting guests stay here for free was not her best idea," he said. He shook his head and laughed.

"What do you mean letting guests stay for free?" said Patrick. He looked at me. "You're not staying for free, are you, Todd?"

"No," I said.

"And we certainly aren't!" said Patrick. "Although I wouldn't be surprised if Dad asks for some kind of refund, to be honest. He hasn't exactly loved this hotel. . ."

Howard fixed his eyes on Patrick.

"You seem to be the most sensible one," he said. "Your dad is a businessman, isn't he? I saw his name on the list of guests."

Patrick didn't react, but Howard continued.

"As the son of a businessman, you must realize that this hotel can't continue like this, don't you? In fact, maybe your father would be interested in investing in the new apartment block I'm intending to build, once this place is flattened, of course. He must be looking to make money. I can get my people to talk to his people and see if I can get him in on the deal."

Patrick's mouth twitched.

"My dad doesn't deal with *sharks*," he said.

Howard nodded, a disgusted look on his face. He turned to me.

"So, what have you found so far? It's Todd, isn't it? Go on, tell me what it is you're up to and then maybe Scout and her mum will keep a roof over their heads."

Laurie suddenly stepped forward. "Our teacher says that mean people are just sad inside, so that makes you mean *and* miserable!" she said.

Howard laughed.

"I don't think so, little girl," he said. He looked at

the four of us and shook his head. "Anyway, I can see that I'm wasting my time here."

His mobile phone pinged and he took it out of his pocket and read a message.

"It's my lawyers," he said. "They're all ready for when your mum signs, and she will sign, mark my words."

"Why don't you go away with your stupid lawyers and stupid contract and never come back!" said Scout furiously.

Howard pressed his palms together and rested his fingers on his lips as he stared at the floor. Then he looked up.

"You do know where you'll end up if anything puts this sale in jeopardy, don't you?" he said.

Scout grinned. "Er, let me think about it. Living happily ever after?" she said sarcastically.

Howard put his head on one side.

"I'll walk away from this dump of a hotel and I'll take all of my money with me," he said. "I'll leave you here, all on your own with your huge, leaking roof, your dodgy electrics and weeks and weeks of no bookings."

Scout frowned. Her eyes flickered to mine, then Patrick's. There was panic in her face.

"Oh, you did know that, didn't you?" said Howard. "After these poor guests have left you have absolutely no bookings at all for the Paradise Hotel. Not one."

Scout swallowed but still didn't reply.

"You haven't given this much thought, have you?" he said, his bottom lip protruding like a toddler's. "Poor, poor Scout. Where will you live when the bank repossesses your precious hotel, eh?"

"W-what do you mean?" said Scout.

"Your hotel is finished. The debts have mounted up around this place so much I'm surprised you can see out of the windows! You've been too busy running around in those ridiculous goggles to see what is going on right under your nose," he said. "I have reached a hand out to your family and it is stuffed full of real cash. My offer will mean that you won't end up on the street. There'll be no more offers. You will be homeless, Scout. Do you understand?"

Scout nodded slowly.

"Good," said Howard. He reached towards the wall and took the painting. "I'll look after this for now," he said. "It's clearly of importance. I'll get my team on it right away and find out for myself what it is you're up to."

Howard held the painting against his chest. There

was a label on the back but I couldn't make out what it said. I could see that Patrick was trying to take a look as he was standing closest to him. I needed to distract Howard so that he didn't notice.

"Did you say that the hotel would be yours soon?" I said. Howard nodded.

"Well, soon isn't *now*, is it? So that painting still belongs to Scout and her mum. I think you should give it back."

"Actually, I think we should let him take it," said Patrick. "I don't think we can argue. The painting is his."

He gave me a sly wink. Whatever he'd seen on the back of the painting was enough that we could let it go. But Scout didn't know that.

"What are you talking about, Patrick? This hotel is *not* Howard Knife's. And that painting is *not* his property," she said.

I tried to catch Scout's eye but she was too busy glaring at Howard.

"I think I'll just let you kids argue amongst yourselves," said Howard. "In the meantime, you can call this a deposit. Your mum's seen sense now, but who knows what stupid decision she might make next?"

Scout's jaw dropped open and I saw her tense her fists. I put my hand on her arm.

"See you later, kids," said Howard. His mobile phone began to ring and he tucked the painting under his arm and walked out of the room.

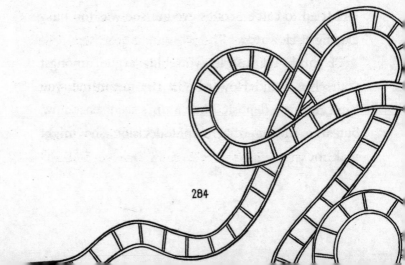

CHAPTER THIRTY-THREE

"This isn't how escape rooms work."

As soon as the door closed, Scout turned to Patrick.

"WHAT WERE YOU THINKING?!" she bellowed. But Patrick was smiling, although also holding his hands up, just in case she lurched towards him.

"It's fine! It's fine! The painting is worthless," he said. "I saw the label! Oh, it's brilliant."

"What is brilliant?" said Scout, desperate to know. "Tell us!"

Patrick grinned. "On the back of the painting was its title," he said. "I can't believe I didn't think of it before, but the subject of the painting gave it away!"

"A red fish?" said Laurie. I was as confused as she was.

"No!" said Patrick. "The title of the painting is *A Red Herring*! Whoever put it there has a great sense of humour. It was their idea of a joke. And a brilliant one it was too!"

Scout shook her head in disbelief.

"I don't get it," said Laurie. "What's a herring? And why is it red?"

"A red herring is a misleading clue!" I said. "I think it has something to do with smoked fish and using their smell to distract a dog chasing a rabbit. Or something like that anyway. We learned about red herrings when we were reading a mystery story at school."

Scout looked relieved.

"So the painting doesn't have anything to do with the clues at all?" said Scout.

"Nope," said Patrick. "But it'll only be a matter of time before Howard realizes the same thing."

"Yes, we've got to hurry! Mum will be back now and Howard will be pestering her to sign. We've got to find something else to do with the sea!" said Scout.

"Why don't we split up and search different areas

of the room?" I said.

"Yes," said Patrick. "Scout? You check the wardrobe in case we missed anything. Laurie? Check under the bed again, can you?"

Laurie dropped to her knees and peered into the gloom, knocking the bedside table as she did.

I checked behind the tall curtains and then under the desk. "Nothing here," I said.

"There's only shoes under here," called Laurie.

"Hang on," said Scout. "Look. There's something on top of the wardrobe."

I was the tallest and I could just make out the edge of some kind of box. I grabbed the chair in front of the desk and carried it over to the wardrobe, then climbed up.

"It's a suitcase!" I said. I reached for the handle and pulled it towards me. I lifted it down. It felt very light.

"It's got a combination lock!" said Patrick. "Quick. Put it on the bed so we can try the numbers from the tidal abacus. You do it, Todd."

The brown suitcase was dusty and there was a luggage label attached to the handle. It said "Ms E. Patterson" in the same handwriting as the clues.

"It's so light. I don't think there's anything in it," I

said. "But there are two combination locks. We need to put in three numbers."

"Try the numbers we found!" said Scout. "28 and 1."

There were two combination locks and I twiddled the small dials to 281 on both sides. I tried the clasps but nothing happened.

"Try the other way around," said Patrick. "Put in 128. That should do it."

I twirled the dials around again and stopped at 128. "Here goes," I said, and then I pushed the buttons and the clasps popped open.

I gently opened the lid. Inside was a piece of paper. It was some sheet music.

"It's music," I said. I read the top of the sheet. "Moonlight Sonata by Beethoven. And there's something written in pencil on the top. It says ... 'ballroom'."

Patrick huffed.

"Well, that's stupid," he said. Scout shot him a look.

"Why? What's stupid about it?" she said. "The music must be the next clue, obviously! And it sounds like we need to go to the ballroom."

Patrick shook his head.

"But that's not how it works!" he said. "All of the clues are supposed to stay in the room. I know that Todd took the book and that werewolf bloke told us about the abacus, but we didn't *need* to leave the room to know that." Patrick sat on the bed with a sigh. "This isn't how escape rooms work."

He really did seem to be disappointed.

"Patrick. I think you're forgetting that this isn't an escape room. It's a series of puzzles created by a brilliant mind, many decades ago. Well before escape rooms were even invented!" said Scout.

Patrick snorted. "Yes, but we shouldn't have to *leave* the room," he said. "That's the whole point."

Scout looked at me. "Todd? What's your opinion?" she said.

"I think it's all really interesting," I said, gesturing around the room. "I've no idea who created all of this, but it's clearly the work of some kind of mastermind."

Scout grinned. "Good," she said. "Let's take that piece of sheet music and go to the ballroom, shall we?"

Scout walked to the other side of the room and stood beside some wooden panelling. Tucking her jet-black hair behind her ear, she grinned, then she faced the wall and pressed firmly in one of the wooden squares. The wall gave a gentle click, then opened like a door.

"IT'S A SECRET PASSAGEWAY!" cried Laurie.

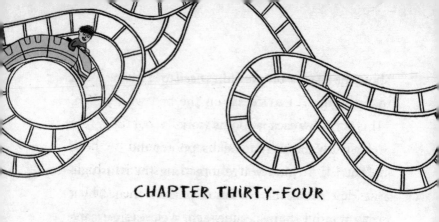

CHAPTER THIRTY-FOUR

"I think it's worth saving."

Scout opened the secret door wider and we hurried over to see what was behind it. There was a stone staircase that twisted around and downwards.

"THIS IS BRILLIANT!" said Laurie. She was so excited. I hadn't seen her like this for some time. I smiled at her.

"How did you know that this door was even here?" I said. "It looks just like a wall!"

"I found some old plans of the hotel," said Scout. "I'm pretty sure Mum doesn't know that I know about them. Come on, I'll tell you more on the way."

Stepping into the stone stairwell was like walking into a fridge. It was freezing.

"They call them secret passageways, but really they were just ways for the staff to get around the hotel unseen by the guests. If you paid to stay in a high-class destination like the Paradise Hotel then the last thing you'd want is to bump into a worker carrying a bundle of dirty towels and bedsheets. I think they stopped using the secret passageways in the 1970s, as they were deemed to be unsafe."

I could see what she meant. Not only was the staircase bone-numbingly cold, but the steps were steep and the bends were awkward. It must have been really hard work for the staff manoeuvring themselves through these tight passageways carrying heavy linen or silver trays piled with food to deliver breakfast in bed.

"Have you explored all of these secret passageways on your own?" said Patrick.

"Yep," she said. It dawned on me then just how lonely it must be living here with strangers coming and going. *And* exhausting with all the jobs she had to do. In fact, I was surprised she was so keen to save the hotel at all. And after what Howard had said about this being their only option, I just wondered if it would be a whole lot easier to just ... give in.

"Have you ever wondered how it might feel to live somewhere else?" I said. Scout stopped abruptly and turned round to look at me. "I mean, just like a normal home where you didn't have to work all the time? And for your mum to not have to worry about the business?"

Scout's face fell and I wished I'd kept my mouth shut.

"I do think about it sometimes," she said. "Especially when I'm at school and Mum has to do everything on her own. But then I walk through the corridors and think about all the history and all the stories that these walls must have heard ... well, *I* think it's worth saving. I know the hotel isn't perfect, but it's my home."

She was quiet for a moment. It was a bit like my family. My dad wasn't perfect, but he was still my dad and I still loved him. Scout carried on.

"Edwina Patterson was my great-great-grandma, and I know it sounds silly because she's long gone and never knew me, but..." She paused for a moment. "I want her to be proud of me. I want to save the Paradise Hotel for her too."

She turned and carried on and we walked down the steps in silence.

I gripped on to the rough rope that had been strung along the wall like a makeshift bannister. It scratched the palm of my hand but I didn't want to let go in case I slipped. I was just beginning to feel dizzy when we arrived on to a flat stone floor. It was another corridor. There were rusty old pipes running along the walls and some very dim lights in rectangular plastic boxes like the kind you get in underground car parks. I looked left and right. Both directions looked identical and very scary.

"This is the cellar," said Scout in hushed tones.

Patrick kept checking around as if he was waiting for someone, or something, to jump out at him. I didn't blame him. This place was giving me the creeps.

"Shouldn't we get going? To the ballroom?" he said.

Scout looked at him for a moment, then nodded.

We followed her along the dark, cold corridor. A few metres along, one of the lights had been smashed and it got even darker.

"Um, how far is it now?" I said. My voice wobbled and I disguised it as a cough.

"Just a bit further," said Scout. We came to the end of the passageway and she turned left, then left again up another steep stone staircase. This staircase didn't have a rope to hold on to and I pressed my hand against the cold wall. Scout was in front and I told Laurie to go ahead of me. Patrick followed on behind. We climbed up and up, the steps twisting round and round until Laurie and Scout stopped.

There was a creaking sound as Scout opened some kind of door at the top. I blinked as light flooded into the stairwell. We carried on up and then out into a room.

"Hang on," said Patrick. "This isn't right!"

The secret passage had taken us to the dining room.

"Oh, what?" said Scout. "I haven't used this passage for a while. We can't have gone far enough. It doesn't matter. We can just—"

Suddenly there was the sound of a very slow hand clap. My stomach dropped when I saw who it was. Howard Knife was walking towards us.

"Bravo," he said, still clapping sarcastically. The painting was face down on a table behind him. "A red herring. No wonder you were happy to give it up so easily. Thought it was funny, did you?"

Patrick snorted and Howard glared at him.

"It sounds to me like you've found the next clue. Am I right?" He was still staring at Patrick. "Where is it then?"

"Say nothing," I said between gritted teeth. We all stayed silent. Laurie pressed up close to me and I put my hand on her shoulder.

Howard turned his attention to Scout.

"OK. I'll level with you," he said to her. "I've played nice. I've tried to show you what's at stake here. Well, you've had your chance. Now the rules are changing. If I don't find Edwina Patterson's treasure then the whole sale is over."

Scout smiled at him and folded her arms.

"That's exactly what I want to hear," she said. But Howard put his head on one side.

"Yes. And I'll take all of my money with me," he said. Scout's smile dropped.

"How do you think your mum will react when she realizes her silly little daughter messed up her only hope of escaping all of her debts? All of her worries? You've seen how anxious she's been, Scout. In fact, I'd say it's making her ill, wouldn't you?"

I saw Scout blink as her eyes filled with tears. It was true. Marianne had begun to look drawn and exhausted.

"Your mum wants to see the back of this place, and I've offered her a solution," he continued. "Surely you realize that, Scout?"

Scout's jaw tensed as she stared at him.

"Mum wants to rescue this place as much as I do,"

she said. "You're bluffing."

"Am I?" he said. "I never lie when money is concerned."

"Scout? Don't tell him!" said Patrick. "Something's wrong here, I just know it."

Scout looked at Patrick and then at me. I knew exactly what I would have done if I was her. I would tell him. But Scout wasn't me. Scout was tougher and a fighter. There was no way she would give away everything that she'd been searching for. But then she turned back to Howard.

"The clue was a piece of music," she began. "The Moonlight Sonata. There you go. It's over. You won."

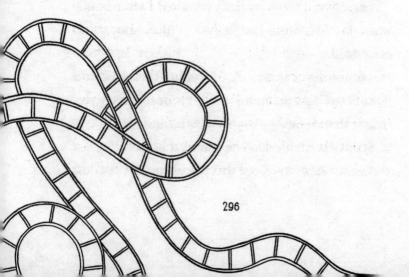

CHAPTER THIRTY-FIVE

"Is that where you were bitten?"

My heart sank. She'd told him! She'd actually told him. Howard's face expanded into a wide grin.

"Beethoven's Moonlight Sonata, eh? I see. Right. It *must* have something to do with ... this!" He rushed over to the piano that William Walters had been playing at dinner time. He looked inside the lid that was propped open, then went to the seat and opened it. Inside were sheets of music. He rummaged through them all. At first I wondered what he was doing, but then I realized that he didn't know that we had the music for the Moonlight Sonata already. It was folded in half and tucked in the back of Patrick's jeans. We looked at each other, but none of us said anything.

"It must be in here somewhere," he said. As he fumbled, the sheets of music dropped all over the floor and he fell to his knees, frantically looking. He turned and sneered at us.

"Do you have it?" he said. "Where is it? TELL ME!"

He got up and stormed towards us.

"We don't have it!" yelled Patrick. "If you can't work out what it means then that's not our problem!"

Suddenly a deep voice boomed across the dining room.

"Who has been messing with my music?"

William Walters stood in the doorway, his shoulders rounded, his head bent forward.

Howard flinched.

"I caught these kids messing around with the piano," he said. Laurie let out a gasp.

"That's not true!" she squealed. "It was HIM!"

William grunted, then walked over to the sheets that were spread all over the floor. Laurie ran over and began to help him pick them up.

Just then Marianne walked in. She was clutching a bundle of papers.

"Mr Knife?" she said. "Can I just go over a few of these clauses with you, please? I'm not too clear on a few things."

She frowned at us, bewildered as to what we were all doing there, then just shook her head as if she didn't have the time or the effort to ask. She looked very, very tired.

"Of course, Ms Patterson!" said Howard brightly. "I'll be right with you."

He trotted across the hall, giving Scout a discreet glare on his way. After he'd left I let out a breath. That man seemed to suck all the oxygen out of a room.

"Are you OK?" I said to Scout. She looked like she wanted to cry, but she quickly composed herself.

"I'm fine," she said. Despite her bravado, I could see she was shaken. Things really didn't look good for Scout and her mum. The three of us went over to the piano, where Laurie and William were carefully replacing the sheet music into the seat of the piano stool.

"Laurie here has been telling me all about what you're trying to do," said William. "The Moonlight Sonata was the clue, I believe?"

"Yep," said Scout sadly. "Patrick has the music. Don't you, Patrick?"

Patrick took the sheet music out of his pocket and then something dawned on me.

"Hang on a minute. We aren't in the right place, are we?" I said. "Howard distracted us by thinking it had something to do with the piano. It said "ballroom" on the music. This is the dining room!"

Scout's eyes widened. "There's a piano in the ballroom too! It hasn't been touched for years."

She looked at William.

"Do you think you can help us, William?" she said.

He seemed to consider it for a while. His face looked just as angry as always, but then he nodded.

"I can try," he grunted.

We followed Scout to the back of the dining room and out through a door in the corner that I hadn't even noticed before. This led down another corridor. At the end were some double doors with scroll-shaped golden handles. Scout pushed the doors open. The ballroom was vast. The floor was wooden and as we walked it felt slightly springy under my feet. There were six large windows that reached up to the ceiling. Each one had a pair of faded yellow curtains which were tied back with giant bows. In one corner there were chairs and tables stacked on top of one another and beside those was a black grand piano, covered in a layer of dust.

Scout rushed over to the piano and put the piece of music on the stand.

She lifted up the piano cover, revealing its ivory and black keys.

"William?" she said. "Do you think you could play it for us?"

William walked over to the stool and sat down. He rested his fingers on to the keys, and began to play.

The music was slow and sad and flowed in a gentle rhythm. William nodded his head and swayed a little as he played. His right hand moved up the keys to reach a higher note, but when he pressed it there was a strange clunking sound. He stopped.

"What was that?" I said. William pressed the key again. Rather than a melodic note, there was another clunk. Patrick gasped.

"There's something in the piano!" he yelled. "The piano key is hitting something!" He ran to the back where the lid was propped up and peered inside.

"Try the note again, William!" he said. It was like he was looking inside a car engine and asking the driver to rev. William pressed the key and it clunked once more. Scout, Laurie and I raced over to see.

"There's something in there!" Patrick said. He

squeezed his fingers between a small gap and brought them out holding a small silver key.

"There must be something else to unlock! In room forty-two!" said Patrick.

"Thank you, William!" said Scout. Laurie ran over to him and gave him a hug. William looked a little taken aback, but then patted her slowly on top of the head. Laurie's face was directly beside his forearm. She stood back up and pointed to the scar that was now clear for all of us to see.

"Is that where you were bitten?" whispered Laurie.

William wriggled his nose at her and his mouth twitched into a small smile.

"Now, that would be telling, wouldn't it?" he said.

"Come on, Laurie!" I said. "We've got to go back to room forty-two."

We made our way back through the ballroom and down the corridor towards reception, and that's when we heard it.

Someone was shouting. And they sounded very, very upset.

CHAPTER THIRTY-SIX

"Our daddy's gone all funny."

Scout, Laurie, Patrick and I stopped in our tracks and listened. The voice sounded desperate and I instantly felt nauseous.

"Have you seen my kids?" said the voice. "I've lost them. Todd has brown hair and brown eyes and he's twelve and Laurie is six and she has blonde hair, kind of dark blonde, and blue eyes. I REALLY need to find them."

My chest tightened as I pictured myself slowly ascending the long climb of a rollercoaster. When we walked around the corner into the hotel reception I knew exactly how I would feel next: like I was plummeting downwards and completely out of control.

Scout's mum was the next voice we heard. "They're fine, Mr Franklin. I've just seen them," she said. "Why don't we just make our way back to your room, shall we?"

I squeezed my eyes together, then stepped out into reception.

"Dad?" I said.

He was wearing what he had been wearing in bed: a T-shirt, boxer shorts and no shoes. He still looked so very tired. I slowly headed towards him, the rollercoaster twisting this way and that in my head. He scratched at the side of his neck.

"Dad. We're here," I said. Dad looked at me and blinked a few times. It was as if his eyes couldn't quite focus properly for a moment, then he seemed to see me.

"Todd!" It was as if we'd been away for months. He rushed towards me and gave me a huge hug.

"I was so worried," he said. I felt his strong arms around my back and tried my hardest not to cry. He let go of me, then scooped Laurie up.

"Daddy, no!" she said. "Put me down. Please!"

Dad gently placed her back down again.

"Oh, Laurie, I'm sorry!" said Dad. "I am just so pleased to see you. I woke up and panicked when I couldn't find you anywhere. Are you both OK?"

"Yes, we're fine," I said. I looked down at his naked feet. I could feel my face burning with embarrassment. "You should go back to bed now, Dad. Don't you think?"

He bit on his lip as if he was thinking about it, but didn't move. Laurie reached up and grasped my hand.

"Daddy, you're in your underwear," she said. "You're not dressed." She started to cry. I looked over at Scout and Patrick, who were standing with Marianne. They all looked concerned about what was going on. Howard was there too, looking really angry but also intrigued as to what was unfolding in front of him.

Marianne stepped towards Dad. She had a really warm smile on her face.

"Mr Franklin, is it OK if we have a little chat?" she said.

Dad looked at her, confused.

"You don't seem yourself and I wondered ... is there anyone I can call for you? Someone who could maybe help you?" she said.

"Help me?" he said. "I . . . I don't know."

He suddenly seemed to realize that we were all looking at him and he looked mortified.

"Dad?" I said. "It's OK. We just want to help you."

He shook his head at me, then turned and stumbled out of reception and down the cold concrete steps. Laurie pulled on my arm.

"Todd! You've got to stop him. *Please*," she said.

I watched as Dad walked across the road in his bare feet and climb over the sea wall on to the pebbly beach.

I turned to Marianne.

"I'm so sorry," I said. "My dad . . . my dad does need help. Can you do something?"

Howard stepped forward. "Excuse me, Ms Patterson. But I really do need to get this signed right now," he said. He waved the contract at her.

"Mr Knife, where is your compassion?" said Marianne. "I have a poorly guest here and I clearly need to help him. OK?"

Howard looked past Marianne and out of the door where Dad had run, then turned back to her.

"I'm sorry, but it *is* a hotel you are running here, isn't it?" he said. "As far as I can tell, it's a hotel and not a hospital." He began to leaf through the contract.

Marianne's jaw dropped and her eyes narrowed.

"I'd like you to leave now, Mr Knife," she said coldly.

"What?" said Howard, laughing nervously. "But you haven't even signed this yet! You said you were going to sign it today and … well, time is running out."

Marianne faced him square on.

"I'm afraid *your* time has run out, Howard Knife," she said. "The Paradise Hotel will never belong to you. I don't know why I was even considering it. You're not going to knock down our hotel and build fancy glass apartments. This is our *home*." She looked over at Scout and smiled, then turned back to Mr Knife. "And we will not be bullied out of it. I want you to leave. Right now."

Howard huffed and fumbled the pieces of paper together.

"Well, in that case. Your chance of escaping your debts has vanished," he said. He held up the contract and ripped it into little pieces. He dropped the pieces on to the floor and stormed towards the door.

"You'll regret this, Marianne!" he said. "You mark my words!"

"It's Ms Patterson!" yelled Marianne. The door swung open and Howard left the Paradise Hotel, once and for all.

"Right, where was I?" said Marianne. She took a moment to look back at Scout, who gave her the biggest smile, then turned back to me.

"Now. Your father," she said kindly. Scout held Laurie's other hand. "Has this happened before?"

I nodded.

"He had some tablets from the doctor in our bathroom cabinet. But he stopped taking them and he said he didn't need them any more," I said. "I didn't want to get him into trouble."

Marianne took a long breath.

"He won't get into trouble, but I will have to call my doctor for advice. And she will probably want to talk to his GP and find out what his treatment has been. Has he been like this since you've been staying here?"

I nodded.

"He sometimes gets really tired and can't get out of bed," I said quietly. "Other times he can be really energetic and excited."

Marianne nodded. "Is there anyone else we can call? How about your mum?"

I explained that Mum was working in Africa and that our aunt was on holiday and that there was no one else.

"I don't want..." I began, but my throat tensed. I didn't want to cry so I took a moment. "I don't want my mum to worry. It's really hard for her to get back from where she's staying. And I don't want to spoil my aunt's holiday either. She's done so much for us and ... and she really needed a break."

Marianne smiled.

"I really understand, Todd," she said. "But I'm sure they would want to know. Don't you? Why don't you contact them and then we'll see from there, OK? I'll give my doctor a call now and then I'll go and talk to your dad."

Marianne walked over to the reception desk and picked up the phone.

Scout and Patrick stared at me and Laurie. I felt crushed. Dad had been behaving so strangely and they had seen the whole thing.

"Are you OK, Todd?" said Scout.

"Yep," I said. "Now you know why my dad hasn't been around. Embarrassing, isn't it?"

Patrick put his hand on my shoulder.

"I know all about dad issues," he said. "Don't worry about it."

"You could have told us, you know," said Scout.

"We would have understood, or tried to. We're your friends." Laurie went over to her and Scout gave her a hug.

"I . . . I just didn't know how to say it," I said. I felt a little lighter for them knowing the truth.

I wondered how Blake and Joe would have reacted if they'd witnessed Dad like this. I didn't think they'd be as understanding as Scout and Patrick, that was for sure.

Marianne came off the phone and headed out of the hotel and across the road. She joined Dad, who was sitting on the sea wall.

"Daddy's feet must be really sore," said Laurie, gulping back more tears. "He needs his shoes!"

"I'll go and get them," said Scout. "Shall I grab some clothes too?"

I nodded. "Thank you, Scout," I said. "There's a pile by his bed." I suddenly felt really tired and my legs felt heavy. She headed off to the stairs. I was so grateful that she was taking charge.

"Is everything all right here?" William Walters was standing right behind us.

"It's our daddy," said Laurie, tearfully. "Our daddy's gone all funny."

William took a step closer to the glass door and

peered through.

"He's not been right for a while now," I said.

"Ah. I see," said William. He was quiet for a moment, watching Marianne talking to Dad as they sat on the sea wall.

"You know," began William. "Sometimes the darkest parts of life happen for a reason. And maybe this is for the best."

I cleared my throat. "I ... I'm sorry ... but I can't see how Dad being like this is for the best?" I said nervously.

William smiled at me.

"No. I can see why you'd think that," he said. "But if he's not been feeling well for a while and he's now ... how should I put it? At the bottom of a deep, dark hole. Then the only way out is to start climbing up, up, up. He can't go any lower. Do you understand what I'm saying?"

I looked at William's eyes with their flecks of yellow as he stared out at Dad. I felt like he was telling me that he knew exactly how Dad was feeling. Maybe he had been through something similar himself?

"I guess," I said.

I heard Scout thundering down the stairs.

In her arms she had Dad's trainers, a pair of

jogging bottoms and a jumper.

"I think I got everything," she said. "I'll take them over."

Scout pushed the heavy door open and ran down the steps, carrying the clothes and shoes.

William sniffed. "If you need me, Todd, you know where I am," he said. I nodded and smiled at him, then he headed across the reception to the stairs.

Scout crossed the road and we watched as Dad slipped on the joggers and trainers. He didn't need much persuading to put them on. When he was properly dressed, Marianne placed her hand on his arm and guided him back across the road, and towards her car.

Scout came back up the steps.

"She's taking him to see her doctor," she said. "Don't worry. I'm sure he'll get help."

I felt my legs trembling so I went over to the scruffy sofa and sat down. The relief that someone was helping us was overwhelming.

Laurie joined me and held on to my arm. "Todd? Is Daddy going to be OK?" she said. I gave her a squeeze.

"Of course he is, Laurie," I said. "The doctor will give him some medication which will help him feel more like Dad again. You'll see."

We sat there, staring into space.

"I know!" said Patrick. "Why don't we go back to room forty-two. It seems a shame to get this far and not find out what is next."

Patrick held up the key that he'd found in the piano when William had played Moonlight Sonata.

"We've still got this, remember?" he said. "I know you're worried about your dad but maybe this might help to take everyone's mind off of it?"

Scout looked at me. "What do you think, Todd? Would you rather wait here?"

"We might find treasure!" said Laurie. She'd already got up off the sofa.

"OK," I said. "But first I need to do something."

I took my phone out of my pocket and started typing a message to Mum and Aunt Lexie. I couldn't put it off any longer. Marianne was right. They would both want to know what was going on.

Hi Mum and Aunt Lexie

I'm sorry to bother you but I need to tell you something. It's about Dad. . .

CHAPTER THIRTY-SEVEN

"I was waiting to see when this would come in useful!"

As soon as we got inside room forty-two, Scout, Patrick and Laurie began to search for a lock that the key might fit. I stood back for a moment and watched these people who had become my friends, still on the hunt for treasure and a solution to the mystery of Edwina's disappearance. Patrick was inspecting the desk. If it wasn't for him and his escape-room theory, we would have never got this far. Scout was checking behind the heavy curtains. Her long black coat swished as she moved around, the goggles perched on the top of her head. She looked fantastic. And then there was my little sister, Laurie. She was on her knees, trying to see if there was anything under the wardrobe. My little sister had proved herself to be a superb mystery-solving companion.

Patrick spotted me watching them.

"What are you smiling at?" he said.

"Just you amazing lot," I said.

Scout raised her eyebrows at me and Patrick snorted. He turned back and crouched down by the drawer of the desk. "This is it!" he said. "It fits."

He placed the key in the lock and turned it.

"Open it! Open it!" chanted Laurie.

Patrick pulled the drawer and we all looked inside.

"There's something written on the drawer!" said Scout.

"What does it say?" said Laurie.

On the wooden base of the drawer was handwriting in spidery black ink.

"It says, 'The carpet hides many things'," said Patrick. We all stared down at the floor. Unlike the patterned carpets in our rooms and the corridors, this one was plain and beige.

"There must be another clue here, right under our feet!" said Scout. "Make sure you search every inch."

I started searching in one corner and made my way along by the tall windows. Then I spotted something in the other corner.

"There's something here!" I said. "A piece of the carpet has been cut out." The others rushed over and I dropped down to my knees. From a distance it looked like a little hole, but close up the shape was defined.

"It's a crescent shape, like a moon!" said Scout. Someone had cut it out, possibly with a knife or a scalpel. I put my finger into the moon-shaped hole and pulled the carpet from the corner. It came up easily, revealing a floorboard with a circular indentation in the middle. I tried to move the floorboard, but it was fixed.

"It's like some weird kind of lock," I said, disappointed. "It looks like something has to fit in the circle to open it."

"And I know exactly what we need to open it!" said Patrick. "I was waiting to see when this would come in useful!" He ran over to the bedside table and came back with the cocoa mug. He placed it on the circle and pressed down, then twisted it slightly. There was a click and the floorboard popped up.

Scout looked at me, her eyes wide.

"This is it," she said. "I think we've found it!"

I took a long, deep breath, then prised the floorboard up. Tucked in the darkness and under the floor was a large brown envelope.

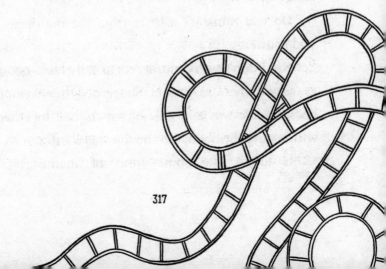

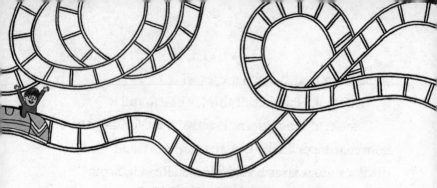

CHAPTER THIRTY-EIGHT

"Here we go."

Scout put the envelope on her knees and took a deep breath. There was something written on the front.

"To whomever it does concern," she read. She looked up at us.

"Do you think it's a letter from the murderer?" said Laurie.

"No, I don't think murderers usually leave notes at crime scenes," said Scout. She ripped the envelope open. Inside was a bundle of papers tied together with a purple ribbon. On the top was a letter.

"It looks like some kind of manuscript,"

said Patrick.

Scout looked at the letter.

"It's dated twenty-ninth of May, 1955. The day Edwina disappeared!" said Scout.

"What does it say?" said Laurie. "Read it, Scout!"

Scout blinked and took a deep breath.

"OK," she said. "Here we go."

She cleared her throat.

"Dear friend, I am thrilled that you have managed to solve the puzzle of room forty-two. It gives me the greatest pleasure to present to you and the rest of the world the manuscript of my next novel, *The Moonlit Mystery*."

Scout paused for a moment and took another look at the thick bundle of papers. On the front was a piece of paper with a typed title:

The Moonlit Mystery
by Edwina Patterson

Scout carried on reading.

"This novel is set in a hotel when a guest disappears on a moonlit night, but things aren't what they seem. I hope the mystery will keep you guessing and take you on many twists and turns . . .

"Now, you may be wondering why I have decided to present the manuscript to the world in this way. Well, the answer is that I am afraid my time is coming to an end. I don't want any fuss or attention. I have made plans to retreat to a quiet place where I will be well cared for, and the rest of the world will see my exit like the mysteries of one of my books."

Scout stopped and looked up at us. "I don't understand," she said. "It doesn't make sense."

"Keep reading!" said Patrick. "I want to know what happened to her!"

Scout carried on.

"My loyal friend and hotel manager helped me to arrange this room as a mystery that mirrors my new novel: the disappearance of a guest and some mysterious clues. . .

"And now a final message to you, dear reader. As I finish my cocoa and before I make my way out of the secret panel and down to my waiting chauffeur, I want to congratulate you on your curiosity, your creativeness and your determination to solve my puzzles. Please accept this manuscript as a gift from me.

Sincerely,

Edwina Patterson."

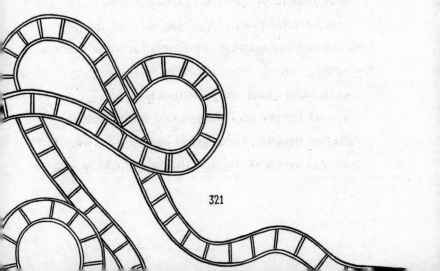

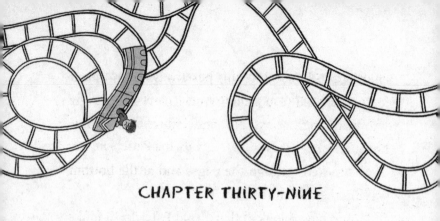

CHAPTER THIRTY-NINE

"Is that the treasure we've been looking for?"

Scout looked up from the letter, her eyes wide.

"A book?" she said. "She left ... a book?"

"Is she not murdered?" said Laurie.

"No, Laurie," I said. "She was old and not very well and she just wanted to go away for some peace and quiet."

Scout looked back at the manuscript.

"I can't believe it! It's an actual letter from my great-great-grandmother. It feels like..." She cleared her throat and I could see this was making her emotional. "It feels like this has always been meant for *me* to find? You know? And I can't believe she wrote another book! No one knows about this, I'm sure!"

She flicked through the pages and at the bottom was another document.

"Can I have a look at that?" said Patrick. "It looks like some kind of contract." Scout passed it to him and he began to read.

"But is that it?" said Laurie. Her nose curled as she pointed at the manuscript in Scout's hands. "Is that the treasure we've been looking for?"

"Yes, Laurie," said Scout. "We've found it!"

Laurie scowled. "But it's just a load of dusty papers," she said.

"It's not just dusty papers, Laurie," I said. "It's a book. An unpublished book by a very famous author."

Patrick was still reading the document and as he read, his eyes lit up.

"Oh, wow," he said. He tapped on a paragraph. "It says here that you need to contact this solicitor and arrange to get the contract signed and then the rights to *The Moonlit Mystery* are yours."

Scout chewed on her lip. "What do you mean, the rights?" she asked.

I was thinking the same thing.

"Does that mean Scout owns the book?" I said.

"Kind of," said Patrick. He reread what he'd been looking at. "When the book is published Scout will get a percentage of the sales. You could be rich!"

Scout's confusion spread to a smile. "Rich?" she said. "Oh, just enough to get the hotel up to scratch would be fine. I don't want to be rich."

Patrick thought that was amusing. He took his phone out of his back pocket and held it up at an angle.

"Let's get a photo of the moment we cracked room forty-two, shall we?" he said. "Get ready!"

Scout pulled her aviator goggles over her eyes and we all started giggling as we posed for the photo.

After Patrick had taken the picture there was a noise I now recognized quite well: the crackle of a walkie-talkie sparking into life.

"Mum to Scout. Mum to Scout. Over," said a voice.

Scout whipped the walkie-talkie out of her pocket.

"Hi, Mum," she said. "Are you back? Is everything OK? Over."

There was a brief pause and then Marianne spoke again.

"Can you come to reception, please? And bring Todd, Laurie and Patrick. Over."

My heart twisted a little. While we'd been in room forty-two I'd managed to push the worry of Dad out of my mind for a few minutes. But now I had to face whatever was next.

"Come on," said Scout. "Let's go and see how he is, shall we?"

We arrived in reception and Dad was standing in the middle of the room with Marianne holding on to his arm. In her hand she had a white paper bag, presumably with Dad's medication inside.

"Hi," said Dad. "I just had to . . . pop to see the doctor and, you know . . . talk about a few things."

He still looked tired and bewildered. Like he had awoken from a coma or something.

"Scout? Why don't you take the others to the dining room?" said Marianne. "I'll just escort Mr Franklin back to his room and then I'll come down and see you."

As Dad walked past, Laurie dived at him and squeezed his legs. He stroked her hair.

"It's OK," he said. "Daddy's OK." He looked at me over Laurie's head. I bit on my lip and he nodded at me.

Marianne came to the dining room as she'd promised and explained everything.

"My doctor spoke to your dad's doctor and you were right, Todd. He shouldn't have stopped taking those tablets. That's why he's been feeling so poorly."

I nodded. "But now what do we do?" I said. "He's still not well, is he?"

Marianne shook her head. "No. It's going to take some time for him to start feeling better, but your doctor is going to get in touch with your dad's psychiatrist, who is going to be the best person to help him. And he's started taking his medication again."

The relief I felt then was immense. Dad was taking his tablets again! Things were going to be better now. He was always a lot better when he took the tablets.

"Can I have your mum's and auntie's numbers?" said Marianne. "I'll need to let them know what's going on and that you're both OK. The doctor has prescribed something to help him to sleep tonight."

I looked back at my phone to see I had lots of messages from Mum and Aunt Lexie. They'd seen my text. I gave Marianne their numbers.

Scout went to her mum and gave her a hug. And then she stood back. Scout was still holding the brown envelope from room forty-two in her hands.

"Isn't it great, Mum?" said Scout, breathless with happiness. "We aren't selling the hotel!"

Marianne sighed deeply.

"For now, maybe," she said. She stroked a strand of Scout's hair away from her daughter's eyes. "But Mr Knife is right, we don't have any more bookings, and as much as you help in the holidays, I just don't know how we'll afford to keep it going just the two of us. We've got no choice, I'm afraid. We'll have to sell to someone."

"But Mum, we don't!" said Scout. "I found something. In room forty-two!"

Scout fumbled with the envelope that she was still holding and pulled out the letter, contract and manuscript.

Just then, Patrick's dad, Roland, walked into the room.

"Is there any food going?" he said. "I'm absolutely famished!" Patrick rushed over to him.

"Dad," he said. "Scout found a contract! We found an unpublished manuscript by this old woman. In *fact* it's that old woman!" He pointed to the large painting of Edwina Patterson who I then noticed had been painted with a slight smile on her lips.

"I reckon it could be worth thousands!" said Patrick.

On the mention of a contract and money, Roland's eyes lit up.

"Can I see?" he said. Scout passed the papers over

to him and he scanned the contract and letter and the looked at the manuscript.

Then he looked up at Marianne.

"I think you've got something here," he said, his eyes wide.

Marianne stared at Roland and Scout.

"What are you talking about?" she said.

"Scout has found an unpublished manuscript by Edwina Patterson in room forty-two," I said. "And there's a contract that means you'll get a share of the book sales!"

Marianne stared at me, unblinking, and then she slumped into a chair and Scout went over and hugged her.

"Isn't it great, Mum?" she said. Marianne patted her on her back. She looked dazed for a moment and looked up at Roland.

"Are you sure?" she asked. Roland nodded.

"Absolutely," he said.

A look of relief spread across her face.

"Oh my goodness. Let's hope Edwina's book really does help us," she said. "Do you think it'll be enough?"

Roland shrugged and then Patrick cleared his throat and stepped forward.

"Excuse me, Marianne?" said Patrick. "I was just wondering ... have you ever thought about using part of the hotel in a different way? I mean ... you don't actually have to use the whole building for guests," he said.

Marianne rubbed her forehead.

"Well, no. I haven't thought about that. It's always been a hotel to me, you see. Why? Do you have any ideas?" she said.

Patrick looked at his dad, who smiled back at him.

"I do," he said, wiggling his eyebrows. "Tell me, have you ever heard of an escape room?"

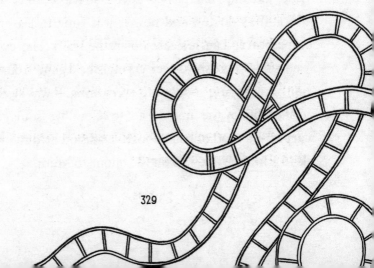

CHAPTER FORTY

"Is this where the tearful goodbyes are?"

Laurie pulled her suitcase behind her as we made our way down the corridor towards the stairs for the last time. Two days had passed since Dad had been to see Marianne's doctor, and now it was time to leave. I helped carry Laurie's case down the stairs. Her eyes were pink where she'd been crying. She'd gone around our room saying goodbye to everything. It was sweet to start, but by the time she got to "Goodbye, squiggly carpet" I'd kind of had enough. Dad said he'd follow us in a minute. He was on the phone to Mum.

We came down the last few stairs and a voice shouted across the room.

"Todd! Laurie!" It was Aunt Lexie. It was so surprising to see her there! Laurie sprinted across the room and dived into her arms.

"Aunt Lexie! What are you doing here? What about your holiday and all the countries?" she said.

Aunt Lexie gave her a kiss on the cheek.

"I didn't mean to spoil your holiday, Aunt Lexie," I said. "I'm so sorry."

"Oh, Todd, between you and me, I couldn't wait to get off!" she said. "I felt sick from the swaying of the boat and some of the people on board just didn't stop talking. You couldn't get any peace unless you were in your cabin. And we didn't have a window so it was like being in a wardrobe or something."

Laurie giggled. I wasn't sure if Aunt Lexie was just saying all of this to make me feel better, but it did.

"Anyway, how's your dad doing? I spoke to that nice lady at reception and she said he's back on his medication now. Is that right? I had no idea he'd stopped taking it," she said.

"Yes, it's only been two days but he seems a little bit better," I said. This time I'd looked at the foil packet and made sure that they were being taken.

Even in that short time Dad had improved enough to eat with us in the restaurant, and after that we'd gone for a long walk along the seafront and skimmed stones into the waves. I'd also video-called Mum and she was on her way back. She wasn't angry with me for not telling her, or with Dad, but she wanted to come home and make sure we were all OK. I was relieved about that too.

"Ah, here comes your dad now," said Aunt Lexie.

Dad walked over to join us.

"Hi, sis," he said. "I'm so sorry."

Aunt Lexie gave him a hug. "It's fine. Honestly," she said. "I got the train here so I'm going to drive you all back in your car, OK? You can sit up front with me and we can chat or you can sleep. It's up to you."

Dad smiled. He looked so grateful to have her there.

"Thank you. I'll hand the key in," he said.

My phone pinged with a message and I took it out of my pocket. Earlier I'd sent Blake and Joe a photo that they'd been so keen to see of my stay at the Paradise Hotel. The photo I'd sent was the one that Patrick had taken in room forty-two. Scout was holding the brown envelope and through her aviator goggles she was staring intently into the camera with a serious "I've-just-solved-a-mystery" expression on her face. Patrick had his arms wide and was pulling a silly face, Laurie was grinning and holding up two thumbs and I was just laughing and looked very, very happy.

I read the message.

Blake: Cool! What's in the envelope?! When are you back? You can tell me all about it.

I put my phone in my pocket. I'd reply in the car.

Laurie, Dad and I went over to the desk where Marianne and Scout were waiting. Dad placed the key on the desk.

"Thank you, Marianne," Dad said. "For everything."

"It was not a problem," said Scout's mum. "In fact, I think I should be thanking you. From what Scout has told me, your two were instrumental in finding the manuscript to *The Moonlit Mystery.*"

Dad frowned at us. He had no idea what we had been up to while he was sleeping.

"I'll tell you all about it in the car," I said. Dad went back to Aunt Lexie and Laurie turned to Scout.

"Thank you for the best holiday ever," she said. "I'll never forget you." And then she burst into tears and threw her arms around Scout's waist.

"Oh, Laurie. Don't cry!" said Scout. "Please... Um, Todd? Can you help me here?"

I walked over and patted Scout on the arm.

"Nah, I think you can take this one," I said. "But thanks. Are you going to be OK?"

Scout looked at me over Laurie's sobbing head and she nodded.

"I think we're going to be fine," she said.

"Is this where the tearful goodbyes are?" said a voice. It was Patrick and his dad. Patrick's dad placed the key to their suite on the reception desk.

"I've made some calls," Roland said to Marianne, "and a few of my associates are going to be in touch. They sounded very excited about your proposal for a new look and I think you'll be swamped with investors. Everyone is diversifying these days. And a boutique hotel that hosts murder-mystery weekends and has escape rooms is going to be a huge success. In my opinion, anyway."

"Thank you," said Marianne. "Well, we'll soon see if we can make it work, I guess."

Roland Harris's face stretched as if he was in pain, but then I realized it was actually a smile. He clearly hadn't used those muscles for quite some time.

"And, ahem, I just wanted to let you know that I'd

be very interested in a project like that, so if you're looking for a business partner," he said, passing her a small white card. "Here's my number, so let me know if you'd like to have a ... conversation."

Marianne looked at the card and then at Roland. I got the impression she was trying not to laugh. Considering how rude he'd been throughout his stay I didn't think she'd accept.

"I'll bear that in mind. Thank you," she said. He nodded as if he'd done her the best favour in the world.

"Come on, Patrick," he said. "Let's get on the road."

"I'll see you in the car, Dad. I won't be long," said Patrick. He turned to us.

"I guess this is goodbye then," he said. Laurie had let go of Scout now but started sniffing again.

"Goodbye, Patrick," she said. "I'll never forget you."

Scout punched him on the arm. "Yeah, thanks, Patrick. If it wasn't for you starting this whole escape room thing, then I think we'd be in a very different situation here, don't you?"

Patrick shrugged and turned a bit pink. He faced me.

"See you later, Todd," he said. "Text me once in a while, eh?"

"For sure," I said. And I knew that I would.

Laurie and I made our way across the reception to

where Aunt Lexie and Dad were waiting.

Dad put his arm around my shoulders.

"Ready to go home now?" he said. I turned back and gave the Paradise Hotel one last look.

"Yes, Dad," I said. "Let's go."

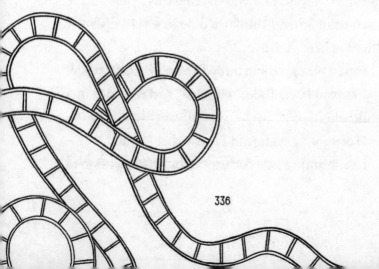

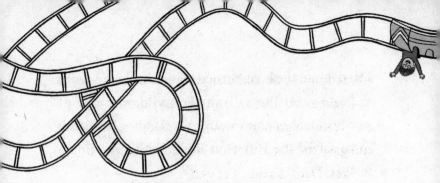

CHAPTER FORTY-ONE

"Congratulations, Team Franklin, you did it!"

Laurie fiddled with the padlock until the numbers read 2498. As soon as they were in position the lock sprang open.

"Take it off and open it!" said Mum. "Quick! What's inside?"

The small wooden box was lined with green velvet, and inside was an ornate silver door key.

"That's it!" said Dad. "That's the final key! Go on, Todd. You do it."

I took the key and we all raced over to the door. I

fitted it into the hole, turned it and the door opened.

"Congratulations, Team Franklin, you did it!" said Scout. She came towards us, clapping her hands. "You solved the Patterson Room with two minutes to spare!"

"That was just brilliant," said Mum. "Can we do another one?"

Scout smiled at her. "I'm sorry, Mrs Franklin, but our other two rooms are fully booked today."

"Oh," said Laurie.

"I can probably give you a slot later during your stay," said Scout, with a wink. "Why don't you go for a swim? The weather is great and the beach is looking really beautiful today!"

"Yay, swimming!" said Laurie. "Come on, Mum!" She started pulling on Mum's hand. Mum laughed.

"All right, I'm coming," said Mum. She looked back at me and Dad. "Are you two coming?" she said.

"Of course!" said Dad. He looked really happy. This was the first time we'd been away as a family since Mum and Dad split up. I was sharing a room with Dad, and Mum was with Laurie. I knew they weren't going to get back together or anything, but it was still really nice to be together.

"I'll see you there, if that's OK," I said. "I just want

to have a quick chat with Scout."

"Sure," said Dad.

"See you soon, Todd," said Mum. Laurie grabbed both of their hands and swung them back and forth as they headed off.

I turned to Scout.

"This place is great," I said. "The Paradise Hotel is so cool now."

Scout shrugged. "It always was cool, Todd," she said. "It's just that some people couldn't see it."

"Have you heard from Patrick? Is he doing OK?"

"Yep. His dad helped Mum with her business plan and securing the money for the renovations. He keeps calling about investing so I think they might be paying us a visit soon," she said. I smiled. That was great news.

We walked out of the escape room area to the corridor where there was a desk for people to register. Behind the desk was William Walters. I stopped and stood to one side.

"And how is the werewolf doing?" I whispered to Scout. Scout looked over at William, who was peering down at the booking sheet. They'd even found him a job in the new business.

"He's fine," said Scout. "He's helped Mum out

with so many jobs, we couldn't do without him. He resets the puzzles in the rooms after the guests have finished. Mum said that my Grandma let him stay many years ago when he had nowhere to go."

"So he was homeless?" I asked.

"Yes, I think so. She gave him a room and in return he did some odd jobs and played the piano in the evening. And he's never left. That's why Howard Knife was so rude about Mum letting guests stay for free. He just didn't understand anyone who had compassion in their heart."

"So, he's not a werewolf after all?" I said.

"Who knows?" said Scout with a laugh in her voice.

William looked up at us as we walked closer. I wondered if he remembered me as a guest who'd stayed all those months ago. He frowned in his usual, scary way.

"I think you've got something there," he said, holding out his hand. "The key?"

I looked down.

"Oh yes. Sorry," I said. I held out the silver door key that I'd used to unlock the escape room to get out. I dropped it into his palm, but as soon as the key hit his skin he flinched and pulled it away sharply. It was as if the silver key had singed his skin. Hadn't

Patrick said that silver was the only thing that could hurt a werewolf?!

William Walters looked at me, and then at Scout, and gave us both a wink.

Scout grinned at me.

"Come on," she said. "I'll race you to the ballroom. You must come and see what we've done!"

I smiled back at her and we both began to run.

DON'T MISS THESE OTHER
BESTSELLING, AWARD-WINNING
BOOKS BY LISA THOMPSON

*A story of finding friendship when
you're lonely, and hope when
all you feel is fear.*

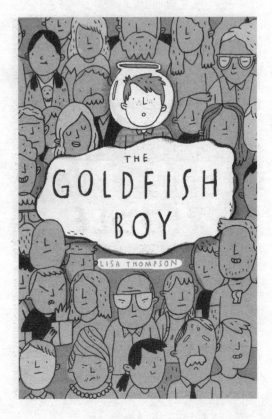

"A great cast of characters and an intriguing
mystery – I loved it!"
**Ross Welford, bestselling author
of *Time Travelling with a Hamster***

An old, abandoned house hides a
secret within its walls...

"Pure, breathtaking genius"
**Maz Evans, bestselling author
of *Who Let the Gods Out?***

A story of family, friendship and finding your place in the world.

"Brimming with Thompson's characteristic warmth and wisdom" *The Bookseller*